PRAISE FOR

# THE SORCERER OF PYONGYANG

"Suspenseful . . . meticulously researched . . . entertaining."

—*San Francisco Chronicle*

"Expert, engrossing . . . a remarkable bildungsroman . . . A cleverly imagined tale of psychic repression and escape from it."

—*Kirkus Reviews* (starred review)

"Humorous yet insightful . . . This entertains and edifies in equal measure."

—*Publishers Weekly*

"Reading *The Sorcerer of Pyongyang* is an informative and entertaining way to learn about North Korea. Theroux's painstaking research intimately reveals the workings of North Korean society, in the public and private spheres . . . [Theroux] writes with intelligence, compassion, and an occasional quiet lyricism. Most crucially, the novel powerfully embodies the plight of North Koreans in the state's vast shadow."

—Krys Lee, *The Guardian*

"A compulsively readable tale, all the better for being set in one of the most secretive countries in the world. Marcel Theroux captures the extraordinary atmosphere of North Korean life with wit and insight."

—Michael Palin, author of *North Korea Journal*

## ALSO BY MARCEL THEROUX

*A Stranger in the Earth*

*A Blow to the Heart*

*Far North*

*Strange Bodies*

*The Confessions of Mycroft Holmes: A Paper Chase*, published in the UK as *The Paperchase*

*The Secret Books*

평양의 마법사

# THE SORCERER OF PYONGYANG

A NOVEL

MARCEL THEROUX

WASHINGTON SQUARE PRESS

ATRIA

New York London Toronto Sydney New Delhi

ATRIA

An Imprint of Simon & Schuster, Inc.
1230 Avenue of the Americas
New York, NY 10020


Originally published in Great Britain in 2022 by Corsair



First Washington Square Press/Atria Paperback edition October 2023

WASHINGTON SQUARE PRESS / ATRIA PAPERBACK and colophon are trademarks of Simon & Schuster, Inc.



Interior design by Jill Putorti

Manufactured in the United States of America

1 3 5 7 9 10 8 6 4 2

Library of Congress Cataloging-in-Publication Data is available.

ISBN 978-1-6680-0266-7
ISBN 978-1-6680-0267-4 (pbk)
ISBN 978-1-6680-0268-1 (ebook)

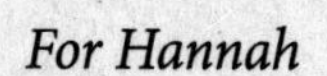

*For Hannah*

# THE SORCERER OF PYONGYANG

# THE MYSTERIOUS BOOK

One Sunday afternoon towards the end of September 1991, a heavyset forty-seven-year-old man with thick glasses and unruly dark hair took his seat on an Ilyushin jet painted in the handsome red and white livery of the North Korean state airline, Choson Minhang.

The man's name was David Kapsberger, and he was about to fly to North Korea as part of a twenty-strong delegation of radical academics and trade unionists.

As a haze of dirty smoke obscured the skyline of Beijing visible through his window, Kapsberger removed his spectacles and dabbed his face with the warm towel offered by one of the eerily composed female flight attendants. The long hours of travel from his home in London had left Kapsberger feeling worn out. His clothes had suffered too. His lightweight summer suit was crumpled and bore stains from a coffee he'd spilled on himself in the transit lounge at Sheremetyevo Airport.

Across the aisle of the plane, luxuriating in the novelty of an entirely empty row, sat his son, fourteen-year-old Fidel Olatunji-Kapsberger. Fidel had been forced to accompany his father on the trip, which he was fully expecting to find pointless and dull. For the first forty minutes of the two-hour flight, he buried himself in a book, but as the plane crossed into the airspace of the Democratic People's Republic of Korea, Fidel glanced out of the window and found himself bewitched. The mountainous landscape that broke through the clouds beneath him seemed somehow prehistoric and mysterious, like a version of the imaginary world in the fantasy novel that he was reading.

After a sudden descent and an abrupt landing that left the tour party shaken, the passengers made their way down the boarding ramp and towards the boxy Soviet-style terminal.

From the roof of this building an enormous floodlit portrait of the country's Great Leader, Kim Il-sung, smiled lovingly out across the concrete airstrip, which still radiated warmth after a day of autumn sunshine.

Dusk was falling on the low wooded hills that surrounded the airport. The stillness was strangely oppressive. An unsettling silence enveloped the visitors as they shuffled into the arrivals hall, which was austere and cavernous, and smelled faintly of detergent.

The elder Kapsberger was an American citizen who had emigrated in the sixties to avoid the draft for the Vietnam War. He'd begun a new life in England as a graduate student in the political science department at the London School of Economics. Now he was a full professor and the world's leading English-speaking expert on Juche thought, Kim Il-sung's unique philosophy of Marxist self-reliance. However, the professor's expertise was wholly theoretical; this was his first visit to North Korea. And, like all foreign visitors entering the country for the first time, he felt a thrilling combination of fear and curiosity as he handed over his US passport for inspection.

The fluorescent lighting inside the glass booth was tinged an unearthly shade of orange. It made the immigration officer look like a waxwork in a vitrine. Only his eyes moved, as he lowered and raised them repeatedly in order to compare the photograph in the passport with the reality of the rumpled man in front of him. Behind his impassive face, he was calculating whether Kapsberger was what the government euphemistically called "an impure element." The professor's unruly hair, dirty suit, and US citizenship tipped the scales in favor of further investigation.

As the officer waved Kapsberger through, he pressed a concealed button under his desk to ensure that the customs men would search the professor's luggage with extraordinary care.

The customs men were looking for anything that might confirm the immigration officer's hunch: including, but not limited to, drugs, precious metals, fissile or radioactive material, pornography, Bibles, subversive literature, weapons or bladed articles, and financial instruments of a value above ten thousand dollars. Needless to say, the professor had none of these things. Finally satisfied, the inspectors left him to repack his ransacked suitcase and join the tour group, to the relief of Fidel, who had been waiting anxiously, having been waved through customs with his own bag unsearched.

Over the subsequent week and a half, the delegation was shown around model farms, a granite quarry, a sewing-machine factory, a youth center containing many preternaturally talented child performers, the Pyongyang Children's Foodstuffs Factory, and Kim Il-sung University.

Although they were all broadly sympathetic towards the tiny nation's eccentric experiment with socialism, none of the visitors was comfortable with the ubiquitous propaganda that claimed virtually divine status for the Great Leader. At the same time, they understood that airing these doubts or betraying any hint of mockery would only make life difficult for their North Korean hosts, all of whom wore tiny gold badges over their hearts bearing the Great Leader's image.

The visitors attended the Mass Games in Kim Il-sung Stadium, climbed the Tower of the Juche Idea from whose viewing platform Pyongyang resembled a diorama of gray matchboxes, spent two days at a beach resort in the seaside town of Wonsan, and were treated to a series of long drunken meals by their hosts. Apart from an argument one evening with the minders when a representative from the National Union of Mineworkers finally ventured a criticism about the cult of personality that surrounded the Great Leader, the tour was uneventful.

However, in an act of forgetfulness that was to have enormous repercussions, Fidel left one of his belongings in the room at the Songdowon Hotel in Wonsan that he had shared with his father.

This was a hardback copy of the *Dungeon Masters Guide*, the core rule book for a popular role-playing game called Dungeons & Dragons that was one of Fidel's passions. The cover depicted a giant red troll abducting an almost naked blond woman. This image would certainly have resulted in the book's confiscation on arrival in Pyongyang, had the customs officials not been preoccupied with the moral degeneracy implied by David Kapsberger's grubby suit and shaggy hair.

A maid, Kim Bok-mi, who found the rule book under the bed when she was preparing the hotel room for a visiting Soviet astrophysicist, was alarmed by the cover. She assumed it to be some form of American propaganda and handed it in to the hotel manager, with many words of apology.

For several days the hotel manager, a man in his late forties called Jon Chol-ju, kept the book in the bottom drawer of his desk. From time to time he would take it out and leaf through its pages while smoking the strong mentholated foreign cigarettes that were one of the perks of his job. Mr. Jon was an educated man who spoke a number of languages, including English, but the book must have been a puzzle to him. It wasn't a genre he recognized. Some of the illustrations were clearly decadent, but they weren't explicit enough to be usefully pornographic. Eventually he consigned it to his lost property collection.

In fairness, the book and the activity it described baffled many of its readers, even outside the Democratic People's Republic of Korea. It contained the rules for a complex game of make-believe set in a world of medieval technology, monsters, and magical powers.

When Jon Chol-ju died of a heart attack a short time later after a drinking binge, the new hotel manager, in an act of largesse, allowed the staff to choose one memento each from among the objects in the late manager's lost property cupboard.

The choices were made in order of seniority. The hotel employees quickly cleared the cupboard of anything edible, wearable, or of obvious value. One of the kitchen staff, a junior chef named Cho So-dok who had recently joined the hotel after ten years of military service, was the last to pick. He was left with two possibilities: a pennant from the 1980 Moscow Olympics or the mysterious book.

It took him a while to make up his mind.

His eyes kept stealing enviously towards the half-empty bottle of Japanese perfume in the hand of the chambermaid who had chosen before him.

On the walk home, he began to have misgivings about his choice. Flipping through the book's incomprehensible pages, he chided himself for not having taken the pennant. When he got back to the apartment he shared with his wife and young son, he dumped the book in a closet containing bedding and more or less forgot about it.

This is how it turned out that, sometime during the summer of 1995, Cho So-dok's eleven-year-old son, Cho Jun-su, stumbled across the book while he was fetching a mattress for a visiting relative.

It was a moment that Cho Jun-su would replay in his imagination for the rest of his life. In years to come, he would joke that it was like a celestial object falling from the sky to be discovered by some bewildered nomad and made the centerpiece of a new religion.

First, a heavy thunk drew his eye to the sight of the book on the floor. As he picked it up, he was immediately arrested by the extraordinary scene depicted on its cover. An enormous horned red giant was holding a naked woman in one hand and a massive sword in the other. The woman fought vainly to break free, but her tiny sword was useless against her supernatural foe. In the foreground of the picture with their backs to the viewer, a knight and a sorcerer, dwarfed by the red giant, also struggled to overpower him. The odds seemed overwhelmingly stacked against them. The knight had already lost his balance and was staggering. But even as defeat seemed almost certain, there was an unearthly light gathering in the sorcerer's raised left hand. It was a magic spell. In that terrible moment of jeopardy, it promised at least a small hope of victory.

Opening the book, Jun-su stared uncomprehendingly at the name of Fidel Olatunji-Kapsberger inscribed on the fly-leaf in both an elaborate cursive script and Elvish runes. He touched the smooth pages with an awestruck hand. Only volumes of *The Life of Kim Il-sung* were printed on such fine white paper. Over the subsequent weeks he would puzzle in secret over the cover, calculating and recalculating the adventurers' chances of victory. He would lose himself in the book's illustrations: scenes of combat, alluring heaps of treasure, scaly dragons, lovingly rendered weapons, the cozy bonhomie of taverns. And he would stare hopelessly at the incomprehensible print on its pages for a clue to its meaning. Despite not understanding a word of it, he felt mysteriously blessed by the book's arrival.

The book's closest equivalents in Jun-su's world were the graphic novels printed by the state publishing house. These could be found on a handcart that was usually parked outside Wonsan Station, arranged in a spectrum of desirability from the tattiest to the most pristine.

The comic books' hand-drawn frames told dramatic stories of space exploration, the strife between feudal monarchs, man-made climatic disasters, and beehives menaced by hostile wasps. They had exciting titles like *General Mighty Wing*, *The Crystal Key*, and *The Blizzard in the Jungle*. And yet, whatever its outward form, each of these stories was essentially the same, a variation on a theme that every citizen knew only too well. The drifting spaceship, beleaguered kingdom, beehive, and jungle research station were all recognizably North Korea, a small country threatened by outside forces and facing a severe economic crisis after the breakup of its biggest ally, the Soviet Union. Just like the North Korean people, the cosmonauts, leaderless knights, scientists, or worker bees were compelled to fall back on their own courage and resourcefulness. Somehow, in every case, the recipe for achieving success against the odds turned out to be identical: self-sacrifice, teamwork, and obedience. The message of each story was to adhere to the ideal of Juche, the philosophy of self-reliance that had been discovered by the brilliant leader, the savior of the nation, Kim Il-sung, whose death a year earlier had been followed by two weeks of national mourning.

In case the parables weren't clear enough, there were mottos written into the margins of the comic books: "Be sure to build a strong fence when there are jackals outside"; "One's honor is harder to keep than it is to earn"; "An old enemy is still an enemy."

The political messages might have been ham-fisted, but the stories were engaging and the illustrations lively. The owner of the cart did good business, lending the comic books for a few chon per half hour to be read on the spot by customers of all ages.

People were eager for diversion of any kind. The nineties were years of famine in North Korea. It was a period of collective suffering that would come to be known as the Arduous March.

Since the collapse of the Soviet Union in 1991, North Korea had faced enormous hardship. Things had got worse after Kim Il-sung died and his son, Kim Jong-il, began leading the country. Torrential rains in June 1995 destroyed the rice crop. The system through which most citizens received their food rations collapsed. Coupons were handed out as usual for rice, cooking oil, meat, and the occasional gray slab of frozen pollock, but when citizens turned up to exchange the vouchers for food at the state-run distribution centers, they were told the shelves were empty. No explanation was given. Government propaganda urged people to conserve food by eating only twice a day—but even that, for many, became impossible.

At school, Jun-su's classmates began to starve. The first signs of it were listlessness and inattention during lessons. A few pupils fell asleep at their desks and were chided by the teachers. Malnutrition lightened the hair of the poorer students and swelled their feet and ankles. People with glassy eyes moved slowly through the streets of Wonsan. Starving workers dismantled the machinery in their factories and tried to exchange it for something to eat. Rice, the staple crop, had disappeared entirely. Outside the city, groups of foragers searched for edible roots and weeds. Children dropped out of school to help their parents scavenge. Scant meals of ground corn porridge were bulked out with traditional famine foods: bentonite clay, poplar buds, acorns, sawdust, elm bark, and thistles. But while these might fool the stomach for a while, they couldn't supply enough calories for survival. Corpses began to appear in the streets and in the entryways of apartment buildings. Some families starved to death together in their homes; singletons gravitated to the railway station to die. There were so many bodies that they had to be stored in piles and collected by truck for disposal in unmarked graves. Rumors abounded of women and children being sold into servitude across the Chinese border, and even of cannibalism.

Jun-su understood that he was lucky. He wasn't part of the country's elite, who were insulated from the suffering. But his parents, Cho So-dok and Kang Han-na, were resourceful. His mother had taken advantage of a government scheme that encouraged citizens to raise pigs. Han-na had to give a few pigs in each litter to the government, but was allowed to keep or sell the remainder. When the time came to butcher the animals, the neighbors formed a queue around the block to buy meat, head, trotters, brain, fat, organs, and congealing blood.

Jun-su's father was also in a privileged position. As a source of vital foreign currency, the hotel where he worked not only remained open, but was guaranteed a supply of food. So-dok would have been risking his life to take anything from the hotel kitchen, but because he was fed at work, there was more food to go round for Jun-su and his mother. Most days Jun-su ate two dispiritingly bland meals of soup, maize porridge, and the occasional fish. He was often hungry, but he didn't starve, unlike many of those around him. At night, the distant cries of hungry children broke the still air like a chorus of frogs.

The teachers suffered too. During a math class one day, Kang Yeong-nam, a dapper man in his fifties with a reputation as a disciplinarian, sat down suddenly in the middle of the room and turned pale. He gazed stupidly around him until the lesson ended and the baffled pupils filed out of class. Later, Jun-su saw Teacher Kang being helped to the sanatorium.

That evening, seated under the precious single bulb that had been a personal gift from the Dear Leader, Kim Jong-il, Jun-su asked his mother if he could bring some extra food to school for Kang Yeong-nam. "Teacher Kang is hungry," he said.

Jun-su's mother exchanged a glance with his father and told Jun-su to finish his food. Talk of hunger made her uncomfortable. It implied criticism of the government. Citizens were careful to speak of *pain* instead of *hunger*. The official causes of death on medical certificates attributed fatalities to food poisoning rather than starvation. The state-run media referred obliquely to a "food ration downturn."

Han-na asked So-dok to switch on the radio. The announcer was reporting on the visit of the Dear Leader to a new ostrich farm outside Pyongyang. The Dear Leader had spent several hours touring the site and giving its managers some on-the-spot guidance. The announcer explained that it was an unprecedented and visionary application of the Juche philosophy: a single ostrich egg was the equivalent of twenty-four hen's eggs and could easily feed eight people.

A few minutes later, a truck with a loudspeaker passed the apartment building and instructed its inhabitants to turn off their lights.

Daily life was strictly timetabled. A bell woke the inhabitants of Jun-su's building every morning at five. The noise of its clapper was echoed by a variety of rings and clanks sounding out across the city. Jun-su and his classmates mustered at the assembly point at 7:45 a.m. and were walked to school by their teacher. School lasted from 8 a.m. to 5 p.m. There was school on Saturday mornings too, followed by political instruction and the Daily Life Unity Critique, where the pupils were encouraged to point out each other's shortcomings in order that they might all become better citizens.

Everyone's life was organized around the same significant events. Each April 15, the country celebrated the Day of the Sun that marked the birth of the Great Leader in 1912. Every September 9 was the Founding of the Republic Day. Each autumn, at the festival of Chuseok, Jun-su's family held a feast of thanksgiving before the ashes of their ancestors. And then, a few weeks later, the government would deliver a big ration of cabbages for each family to preserve for the winter. Every October was tree-planting month. The twenty-seventh of December was Constitution Day. And on February 16, the nation celebrated the Day of the Shining Star, the birthday of the Dear Leader, Kim Jong-il.

It never occurred to Jun-su that life could be any different or better than what it was. He was proud to be a member of the virtuous Korean people. He felt lucky not to be a citizen of South Korea, where the people were much hungrier and their ancient culture was held in contempt by the brutal Yankee occupiers. He mourned the Great Leader, Kim Il-sung, who had worked so hard and cared so deeply for his people; he loved his parents, and felt that he loved the Great Leader's son, Kim Jong-il, the Dear Leader, slightly more. In all respects, he considered himself a loyal and lucky citizen of the Democratic People's Republic of Korea.

On the walls of Jun-su's living room, as in every household, hung two portraits: one of the Great Leader and one of the Dear Leader. Han-na dusted them every day with a special white cloth.

The only real free time Jun-su had was on Sundays. Often, when Jun-su's father wasn't working, he took his son fishing from one of the curving concrete breakwaters that lined Wonsan Harbor. Many families fished there, sending their children to gather shellfish and crabs from the shallows, either to eat or to use as bait. Casting with a rod from the shore, it was possible at various times of the year to catch mackerel, whiting, and bream. One memorable August morning, Jun-su's father cast off with pellets of boiled maize, caught two fat bream, and let Jun-su cast again. Jun-su immediately felt the line go tense and the rod buck in his hand. In all, they caught half a dozen fish before they set off home.

As an adult, despite the terrible things he lived through, Jun-su would retain the air of confidence and self-sufficiency that is characteristic of well-loved only children. It makes it easy to picture him, aged eleven, walking beside his father on one of their excursions to the waterfront. Jun-su is carrying the segments of the rod in a bundle over his shoulder, as though he's a soldier marching with a rifle. He's chatting happily about his life at school, sports, military aircraft—one of his passions—and asking Cho So-dok questions about his work at the hotel, and his impressions of the various nationalities who visited it.

"What are the French like, Dad?" he asked as they walked slowly home, their record catch still twitching in the pair of plastic bags that his father was holding.

Cho So-dok was smoking a cigarette—he favored the Chollima brand, named after the famous mythological horse—with the satisfied air of a successful huntsman. "The French had a revolution of their own," he said, "so although they're capitalist pigs, they're not the worst."

The sound of a lorry grew louder as it approached them from behind. Cho So-dok glanced towards it and watched as it passed, on its way to a nearby collective farm. Rations in the countryside had been cut so low that many farmworkers were too weak to bring in the harvest unassisted. The bed of the truck was packed with soldiers, all standing because there was no room for them to sit down. The soldiers who were visible at the rear were wearing full-face gas masks to protect them from the exhaust fumes that billowed behind the vehicle. The masks gave them a sinister and skeletal appearance.

"Who are the worst?" asked Jun-su. He sensed his father was distracted so he asked it again. In truth, it wasn't a sincere question: every school-age child in North Korea knew the answer. The worst were the Yankee imperialists who had waged war on North Korea, who had divided the North from the South, and who had been defeated by the courage of the North Korean people inspired by the Juche idea. Like children around the world, Jun-su just enjoyed hearing the same stories told over and over, and he was priming his father for this one.

Cho So-dok's eyes followed the lorry as the noise of the engine faded into the distance. He pinched the cigarette and put it back into its red packet to smoke later. "Let's not talk about all that shit," he said.

His father's words hit Jun-su with the force of a blow. So-dok was an undemonstrative man and this behavior was deeply out of character. It would never have occurred to Jun-su that his father might be angry for his own private reasons. Jun-su assumed that he had done something wrong. They walked along in silence for a little while. For a moment Jun-su thought he might burst into tears.

Beside the road, a long banner declared: WE WILL SAFEGUARD WITH OUR LIVES THE CENTRAL COMMITTEE OF THE WORKERS' PARTY OF KOREA.

"I'm sorry, son," said So-dok. "Last week they sent a truck to the hotel and took us out to the fields to help with the harvest. We spent three days bringing in potatoes. Your father's not a young man anymore and when he's tired, he gets short-tempered. It's not your fault."

A few hundred meters farther on, as they passed a red-brick complex of apartment buildings, So-dok nudged his son. "Hey, doesn't your teacher Kang live in there?"

Jun-su stared in puzzlement at his father. He had no idea where his teacher lived. He'd never considered the possibility that any of his teachers had a life outside school. In fact, he found it hard to imagine any of them as fully human.

"In that one at the end," his father said. He made a gesture to identify the building he meant. Then, as though the notion had just struck him, he scratched his head and added, "I tell you what: I bet he'd like one of these fish." He looked at Jun-su. Nodding as though approving his own idea, he continued his train of thought: "In fact, you know what would be better than a fish? Let's give him two." So-dok crouched on his haunches and examined their catch. The silver fish-scales gleamed in his sunburned hands as he picked up the fish to inspect them.

He chose two of the biggest bream and transferred them to a single plastic bag, which he exchanged for Jun-su's rod. Jun-su felt the weight of the bag tug on his arm.

"Just go in and give it to him," said So-dok. "And then hurry home."

Jun-su was surprised. It was an odd thing to do. Not that his father wasn't generous, but food was desperately short. He hesitated and looked at his father. His father nodded to confirm the instruction, then paused, as though struck by another thought.

"Hey," said So-dok, hunkering down again and reaching into the pocket of his windcheater. "Take him this as well." He held out the thin plastic bag containing the two or three hundred grams of cornmeal mush left over from the bait balls.

Jun-su took it and set off towards the complex of apartments. He felt excited as he approached the unfamiliar building. He imagined that he was a spy entrusted with an important mission for the Fatherland. Two children were hanging laundry on a line suspended between two spindly trees. One of them called out to ask him where he was going. Jun-su proudly ignored him.

In the foyer of the building—just as in Jun-su's building—was a glassed-in booth where the chief of the building's People's Unit stood guard. In Jun-su's building, this was nosy Kim Song-hwa, a slight yet formidable woman in her fifties with an impressive coiffure, who observed all the comings and goings of the residents and also gleaned information from a network of informants—mainly people who were too old and infirm to do anything but spy on their neighbors.

Here the chief of the People's Unit was a man who was studying an old copy of the *Rodong Sinmun* through a pair of reading glasses held together with old tape. When Jun-su hailed him as "Comrade Superintendent," he raised his watery eyes. Jun-su explained why he had come and the man waved him up to the third floor.

Jun-su climbed the echoing stairwell. The door of Teacher Kang's apartment was open. Jun-su peered inside. He glimpsed a skinny shirtless figure lying at full stretch on a thin mattress. Jun-su coughed. There was no response. He tapped on the opened door and said: "Teacher, I've brought you something." Still no reply. He slipped off his shoes and boldly entered the apartment.

The floor plan of Teacher Kang's apartment was identical to Jun-su's, but the whole place was messier, darker, and suffused with an unpleasant sickly-sweet aroma. Jun-su stood for a minute watching the rise and fall of Teacher Kang's scrawny chest. Once his eyes had adjusted to the dim light, he looked around at his surroundings. There were shelves of books in glass-fronted bookcases, many of them volumes of the Great Leader's writings. Jun-su moved towards them, vaguely hoping that among all these volumes there might be one of the comics he loved. But all he saw was row after row of boring-looking paperback books whose titles he couldn't even understand.

There was a noise behind him and he turned his head. Teacher Kang had opened his eyes and said in a confused and croaky voice: "Plum blossom, is that you?" He sat up and reached beside him for a glass with some murky liquid inside. He swallowed it, belched lightly, and gazed in perplexity at Jun-su.

Jun-su was so nervous that he forgot to bow or apologize for the interruption. He just stuck out a hand with the bag in it and said: "My dad caught you some fish, sir."

"You can tell your father I don't need his fish," said Teacher Kang grumpily, settling back down onto his mattress. "You keep your fish. Now go away, I need to rest."

When Jun-su got home with the fish and did his best to explain to his parents what had happened, it caused a huge family argument. His mother called his father "a clumsy blockhead," and his father skulked off, clearly chagrined. "I was trying to help the old fool. Is it my fault if he's too stupid and proud?" he muttered.

Autumn settled over the coast, bringing strong winds from the East Sea. Jun-su stared hungrily at the orange persimmons among the bare branches of the trees at the collective farm where he and his classmates were sent to work on weekends, harvesting sorghum and fashioning its long stalks into brooms. Nowadays when they went fishing, his father brought an army canteen of hot water for them to sip and fend off the cold.

At the beginning of November, Jun-su woke up one weekday morning with a terrible soreness in his throat. He had no appetite, and in any case it was too painful for him to swallow. His mother stood him by the window in the weak autumn sunshine and peered into his mouth. His tonsils were swollen and marked with streaks of red and white. She told him he was too ill to go to school. Jun-su pleaded with his mother, but he didn't have the energy to protest for long. He spent the day lying listlessly on his mattress. Now and again the distant sound of martial music disturbed the silence; it was broadcast from vehicles and preceded crackly amplified voices urging the citizens to new heights of productivity and vigilance.

The school sent the senior class representative, a boy named Seo Tae-il, to check on Jun-su that afternoon and report back. It was clear that Jun-su was not malingering; he was seriously ill. Keen not to spread infection among the other students, the headmaster approved his absence.

Days passed. Jun-su's health did not improve. Eventually Han-na bribed a doctor to pay a home visit. He said that what Jun-su needed were antibiotics, but there weren't any available. In fact, there were plenty of antibiotics: Chinese-made ones that had been shipped into the country as part of the international aid effort. The doctor was probably lying in the hope of another bribe; he must have been hungry too.

Jun-su began to display stranger and more worrying symptoms. A red and white rash appeared on his lower limbs. His left knee swelled and became unbearably hot; then as that pain diminished, the joints in his right leg worsened. He was feverish and tired, but couldn't sleep. At night he lay awake listening to his heart pounding.

Even after Jun-su's fever abated, he was too fragile to attend school. Seo Tae-il, the class representative, paid another visit. This time he was accompanied by a second boy. They brought a bouquet of Kimjongilia flowers and a card made by Jun-su's classmates that was signed by all of them and said: *We salute Cho Jun-su for the bravery and compassion he has learned from our Dear Leader.*

Jun-su read the card twice and felt his eyes prickle with tears. Seeing the names of his classmates carefully printed inside the card made him feel very sorry for himself. He had been a confident, popular boy at school. The long empty days were wearing him down and he missed his friends. Seeing his tears, Jun-su's mother took pity on him and arranged with Teacher Kang for her son to pay a visit to his classmates.

On the day chosen for the visit, Jun-su and his mother walked to the school building after lunch. As they entered the premises, Jun-su felt a precocious nostalgia for the familiar surroundings. There was the Kimilsungism Study Hall for which special overshoes were required; there was the painted square in the playground where the children assembled for air raid drills; there was the spot where he had raced with his friend Ri Sok-chung and slipped and sprained his wrist. He was snapped out of his reverie by the sound of his mother's voice. She was shouting at him.

"Stop messing about!" she yelled. Jun-su looked at her in horror. And then his whole body gave an involuntary spasm, as though he were responding to a sensation of extreme cold. It was an uncontrollable shudder that started at his feet and jerked his back and shoulders like the cracking of a whip.

At that moment, Teacher Kang opened the door of the classroom, bowed to Jun-su's mother, and motioned them in.

Teacher Kang led Jun-su to the blackboard and asked the class to welcome their comrade.

A chorus of voices yelled a greeting.

Jun-su bowed happily in reply and began a speech of thanks for the card and flowers they had sent him.

That's when the laughter started.

At first it was just one boy tittering behind his hand; soon his fit of giggles spread to his neighbors, grew louder, and swelled into an uncontrollable wave that seemed to engulf Jun-su. He stopped his speech and looked at his giggling classmates in bafflement. He couldn't understand the reason for the laughter.

But it was clear to the class that Jun-su was clowning. His performance was entirely out of character, which only made it funnier still. Jun-su was rolling his head, flapping his arms, and making hilarious spastic movements with his jelly legs.

At the side of the classroom, Jun-su's mother stood in pained silence, her eyes gleaming with tears, her features frozen in a mask of shame.

"Stop this at once," said Teacher Kang sternly. "The next boy to make a sound will be beaten."

Silence fell on the classroom. But try as he might, Jun-su found he couldn't keep still. His rolling and twitching continued.

"The boy is ill," said Teacher Kang. He indicated to Han-na that she should take him home.

Jun-su and his mother walked home in silence.

Back at the apartment, Jun-su felt overcome with tiredness. He slipped off his school uniform and lay down to sleep. When he woke, it was dusk and the trucks with loudspeakers were urging citizens to conserve fuel and electricity in the name of Juche. It crossed his mind that the whole experience at school might have been a humiliating dream.

He heard the front door open. It was his mother. She sat on the end of his mattress and felt his forehead. Her cool hands smoothed his face and hair. "I bought you something," she said, and she laid a comic book beside him and—equally wondrous—a tiny bottle of fizzy melon juice.

It was unfathomable good fortune not just to be able to read the comic book but actually to possess it. It was called *The Amazing Tincture* and it concerned the discovery of a medicine that brought human beings earthly happiness. Unfortunately, the scientists who discovered it were immediately kidnapped by mercenaries working for the US government. They were forced to endure immense privation before they were finally able to escape and bring the good news of their discovery to the grateful inhabitants of earth.

Jun-su read the book so many times that within twenty-four hours he knew every frame of it by heart.

"You need another book," his mother said. Since the visit to the school, she had doted on him for reasons that he knew were painful ones, but he still didn't want it to stop.

"I've got a book," said Jun-su, getting up. He moved jerkily across to the bedding cupboard and slid the mysterious book out of its hiding place.

His mother gazed at its extraordinary cover. "Where did you get this?" she asked sharply. "Did Teacher Kang give this to you?"

"No," said Jun-su, puzzled that she would associate the staid teacher with such an unusual object. "Dad found it. Can you read it to me?"

Han-na turned the book over in her hands and began leafing through its impenetrable pages. As she did so, she felt Jun-su's eyes resting on her. She looked up at his expectant face, made younger and more vulnerable by its heartbreaking twitch. Opening at a random page, she placed her finger on the text. "'Once there was a boy called Jun-su,'" she began.

"Where does it say that?" said Jun-su.

"Do you want me to read it or not?"

Jun-su was silent.

His mother continued: "'He was popular, obedient, loyal, happy, and kind and lived a long life.'"

"That's not a real story," said Jun-su. "Read a proper one."

Han-na turned the pages of the book. "What about this one: 'The Young Lovers'?"

Jun-su made a nauseated face. "Yeuch."

Han-na turned another page. "'The Brave Airman'?"

"Yes!"

Han-na read it aloud. It was the tale of a young pilot called Kim Jo-on who was flying sorties over the mountains in his Tupolev Tu-28 fighter when the plane was hit by gunfire, forcing him to bail out. Lieutenant Kim trekked through the mountains, endured incredible hardship, ate rats, and made shoes out of birch bark, before finally arriving home to a hero's welcome.

"That is the best story I've ever heard," said Jun-su sleepily.

About a week after Jun-su's disastrous trip to the school, Teacher Kang came round to see him.

There was no mention of Jun-su's visit with the fish or of the events that had occurred in the classroom.

"Show me your tongue," said Teacher Kang, seating himself on the floor beside Jun-su's mattress.

After a brief pause, Jun-su stuck his tongue out.

Teacher Kang moved closer, squinted at it, and grunted. "Give me your arm," he said.

Jun-su did as he was told.

Teacher Kang grasped Jun-su's skinny wrist with his left hand and placed three fingers along his forearm. Then he did the same with Jun-su's other hand.

"What are you doing, Teacher Kang?" said Jun-su.

"Lie still," snapped Teacher Kang. "I studied medicine with Kim Bong-han. He was so smart the Great Leader put him on a stamp. If you work hard and do as your teacher says, they may put you on a stamp one day."

Teacher Kang asked Han-na to take off Jun-su's shirt. He appraised Jun-su's torso by eye as though he were measuring him for new clothes, and then he stuck a needle into Jun-su's upper arm. Jun-su immediately burst into noisy sobs. His mother shushed him and he began to sniffle instead. To his horror, beside Teacher Kang lay a small case that was full of more silver needles.

The truth was that after the initial prick, there was no pain. And a few moments later, Jun-su felt his eyelids droop and a wave of relaxation flood his entire body. "Good," murmured Teacher Kang.

Jun-su drifted off into a state of exquisite calm and all his twitching stopped.

Later that evening, Jun-su's mother sat beside him. "Teacher Kang says you're suffering from rheumatic fever," she said. "That's the reason for the twitching."

"Is Teacher Kang a doctor?" asked Jun-su.

"Kang Yeong-nam has done many things. He's had a complicated life. But he knows a lot and he says he can help make you better. He says it's important to do something . . ." Han-na trailed off.

"Something with those needles?"

Han-na said nothing. She had turned her face away and was wiping her eyes. Jun-su felt himself drifting off to sleep again. "Mum?"

The outline of his mother paused at the door to the kitchen.

"Who's *plum blossom*?"

"You're my plum blossom," his mother said. "Now go to sleep. You need to rest."

Teacher Kang began making regular visits to the house. On each visit he applied his needles to Jun-su, who lay on the mattress in pajamas.

At first, Jun-su's mother stood at the doorway watching the sessions, but after a while, she left them alone.

On one of these visits a strange thing happened.

As the wave of relaxation calmed the twitching in Jun-su's body, he felt his eyes close as usual. His breathing slowed and he slipped into the threshold state of consciousness where the boundary between his skin and the universe seemed to dissolve. Dark waves of purple, orange, and red moved across the inside of his eyelids.

Suddenly he became aware that something was plucking at the cotton sash of his pajamas.

He opened his eyes. "What are you doing, Teacher Kang?" he said.

"I'm trying to make you more comfortable," said Teacher Kang. The teacher's voice sounded thick and wobbly, as though an object was stuck in his throat. He coughed to clear it.

Jun-su sat up on his elbows and stared at the teacher's shifty face.

"I just wanted to look at your pepper," said Teacher Kang.

Jun-su gazed at him with incredulity. It was the weirdest thing he'd ever heard.

"Not to touch it," explained Teacher Kang calmly. He paused for a moment as though weighing a thought. "Unless you want me to." He let this suggestion hang in the air for a moment. "There are circumstances where stimulation of the pepper can help increase vital energy," he said. Although the teacher's face was composed, there was something wild and excited in his eyes.

Jun-su glared fiercely at the old man. "Stop it, Teacher Kang," he hissed. "Or I'll call my mother."

Teacher Kang looked at the formidable expression on Jun-su's face. Without a word, he began removing the needles and putting them back in the case.

After the business with the pajama cord, Jun-su wondered whether he'd see Teacher Kang again. He rather suspected not. But then, a few days later, the old man turned up as usual with his case of needles as though nothing had happened.

All the same, Jun-su was aware that their relationship had altered. He and Teacher Kang had a secret and this secret had given him power over the old man. Now he was emboldened to be more direct with him.

This time while they were waiting for the needles to do their healing work, Jun-su didn't close his eyes. "Have you read *The Amazing Tincture*?" he asked.

"A picture book?" said Teacher Kang, as he took Jun-su's pulses.

"Yes," said Jun-su. He showed Teacher Kang the treasured comic book, which he kept beside him.

Teacher Kang flipped through its pages.

"Read it to me," demanded Jun-su, experimenting with a new peremptory tone.

Teacher Kang raised his head from the book and gave Jun-su a careful sideways glance. For a moment, it seemed to Jun-su that he'd gone too far and was about to get a telling off. Then the old man began to read aloud.

Jun-su found himself drifting into the relaxed state that the needles always brought on. Teacher Kang's voice sounded like a wasp buzzing inside a glass. Jun-su became so sleepy that he could no longer concentrate. The buzzing stopped and he grew suddenly alert in case the old man had designs on his pepper.

"The trouble with this story," said Teacher Kang thoughtfully, laying the book aside, "is that we know exactly what is going to happen. Whereas in real life, everything is uncertain."

"I've got a better story," said Jun-su. "It's called 'The Brave Airman.' "

"I know what happens in that one without even reading it," said Teacher Kang. "Does he crash his plane and survive terrible hardship? Is his bravery held up to the people as an example of socialist heroism?"

"There's more to it than that," said Jun-su. "He eats rats and makes shoes out of birch bark." Trying not to disturb the needles in his chest, Jun-su slid his hand under the mattress to retrieve the mysterious book. He passed it to Teacher Kang. "It's in here," he said.

Teacher Kang looked at the book. His face betrayed no hint of surprise at its extraordinary cover. He flipped through the pages and his eyes moved slowly over the text. For a while he seemed to become lost in its sentences. "Where did you get this?" he asked finally.

Jun-su repeated his father's explanation of how the book

had come into his possession, from the moment of its discovery by the chambermaid, Kim Bok-mi.

"Do you mind if I borrow it?" asked Teacher Kang.

"Just remember to bring it back," said Jun-su. "It's mine."

Teacher Kang kept the book for about a week. He told Jun-su he was reading it with the aid of a dictionary, and updated him about his progress, but refused to give any details until he'd finished.

When Teacher Kang returned the book, it was wrapped in a cover of the cheapest plain brown paper, so rough to the touch that it was useless for drawing.

"I covered it for you," explained Teacher Kang. "You'd have to be crazy to walk around with this picture showing. The demon is red. That could get you a visit from the Ministry of State Security. It looks like an attack on socialism."

The secret police of the Ministry of State Security—the *bowibu*—were notoriously tireless in their efforts to protect socialism from internal and external threats. Loyal citizens had nothing to fear from them, of course. But there was always a nagging fear that one might, through panic or foolishness, inadvertently commit an act of treachery. For example, there had recently been the case of a woman who had rescued her children from a burning house, but disloyally abandoned the portraits of the Dear and Great Leaders to the flames. Not everyone had the courage and presence of mind of the heroic schoolgirl martyr Han Hyong-gyong who had managed to tread water while holding two plastic-wrapped portraits above a rising flood until she finally succumbed to exhaustion and drowned.

The possibility that the book was reactionary propaganda worried Jun-su. "*Is* it an attack on socialism?" he asked.

Teacher Kang explained that it wasn't. "And even if it was, surely socialism is powerful enough to survive the attacks of a few reactionary dogs?" His eyes gleamed with a sly mischief. "Didn't the Great Leader himself say: 'If a man does not read the books he wants to because he has been prohibited from doing so, how can he undertake a great cause?' "

"So what is it?" asked Jun-su.

"It's hard to explain in simple words," said the teacher. "It gives the rules for a game of make-believe. All the players choose a different character. You can decide to be a fighter, or a wizard, and you control them during adventures."

"What kind of adventures?"

"There's another player who creates the adventures. This person is in charge of everything and creates a world for the characters to play in."

"Like the Dear Leader?"

Teacher Kang thought for a while. "I suppose so. Except you can be anyone you want in this game. As you play it, you defeat enemies, find treasure, and make friends. You can die, but if you do heroic deeds you can improve your fortune and win honor."

"Like *songbun*," said Jun-su, whose mother had initiated him early into the secrets of his country's caste system.

Teacher Kang was taken aback. "What do you know about *songbun*?" he asked.

"My mother told me it determines a person's destiny." Jun-su was proud to have learned that he was the grandson of a man who had fought against the Japanese and was therefore of the best, most loyal revolutionary pedigree, rather than a member of the wavering or hostile classes.

Teacher Kang folded his arms and seemed to consider this answer in silence.

"What is the name of this game?" asked Jun-su.

"I call it the House of Possibility," said the old man.

On Teacher Kang's next visit, he brought an exercise book and several sets of the split twigs, flat on one side and rounded on the other, that are used for playing the game of yut. He explained that the House of Possibility was usually played with dice, but that he had adapted the rules so they could play with yut sticks instead.

"I will be the game's leader," he said. "You make your character."

By throwing the yut sticks, Jun-su created numbers that corresponded to certain qualities that he wrote down in pencil on a sheet of scratchy brown paper. His character was very intelligent, but neither strong nor agile. However, he was wise and quite attractive to other people.

"The best thing is for him to be a magic-user or sorcerer," said Teacher Kang. "He can learn spells and do conjuring. But first you have to decide whether he is good or evil."

The old man looked him straight in the eye. Jun-su remembered the teacher's furtive fumbling and his whiny voice saying: "I just wanted to look at your pepper."

"Good, obviously," said Jun-su.

"There are different kinds of good," said Teacher Kang. "There is the good that follows orders and rules, and there is the good that sometimes breaks rules in order to be kind."

Jun-su suddenly worried that he was being tricked. Was Teacher Kang laying a trap for him? Would his answer be held up as a mistake at the Daily Life Unity Critique? Would he be punished, as other wrongdoers were, by having to mop the hallways or being made to clean the disgusting toilets?

"You don't have to be good," said Teacher Kang. "It's not real life." And then he added, in a casual voice: "In the House of Possibility, you can even choose to be bad."

Something about the suggestion put Jun-su in a state of high alert. It was a terrifying and yet fascinating idea. "Are there different kinds of bad?" he asked.

"Indeed," said the teacher quietly. "There are many varieties of bad. There is the bad that takes pleasure in pure badness, the bad that pledges obedience to corrupt authority, the bad of the vicious, the bad of the cowardly, the heroic bad of those boys and teachers who—"

"No!" said Jun-su, interrupting the old man. Now he knew it was a test. "I want to be loyal and good."

From now on, after each session with the needles, Jun-su and Teacher Kang played the House of Possibility.

Jun-su's character was a sorcerer called Bong Chon-ju. Teacher Kang began the game by telling a story about a village that had been overrun with skeletons and whose inhabitants, desperate for help, had turned to the magician.

Bong Chon-ju met them in a tavern, but the villagers were too afraid to return to the village with him, and when he got there it was already nighttime.

Teacher Kang described the thatched huts in the moonlight, the eerie outline of a scarecrow, and the wind rustling through the trees.

It was a frightening scene and Jun-su was tempted to send Bong Chon-ju back to the safety of the tavern. Instead, he told Teacher Kang that Bong Chon-ju would tie up his horse, draw his sword, and explore the area.

Teacher Kang showed him a map of the village where he'd drawn the huts, the well, the barns, and the surrounding paddy fields.

"Where do you go first?" asked Teacher Kang.

"This one."

Teacher Kang threw a handful of yut sticks onto the table and did some calculations in his head. "You approach the hut," he said in the low, serious voice he used for explaining the hardest math problems. "But before you get to it, the door swings open with a *bang* and out jumps a terrifying skeleton waving a sword. What do you do?"

Jun-su was shaken by the description. Teacher Kang had deliberately yelled out *bang* when the door opened in such a way as to startle him. Jun-su looked at the list of spells on his character sheet. There were only three because Bong Chon-ju was not yet a powerful wizard. "I cast the spell 'Magic Arrow,'" said Jun-su.

Teacher Kang nodded and threw the yut sticks. "The yellow arrow flies from your fingertips, striking the skeleton in the middle of his grinning skull. He explodes and clatters to the floor in a pile of dry bones."

Jun-su breathed an audible sigh of relief.

It took two evenings for Bong Chon-ju to clear the village of the skeletons. In the final hut, he discovered a trapdoor that led down to a warren of underground tunnels. Clearly, they needed to be explored.

That night, Teacher Kang stayed for dinner and Jun-su's mother served some of her home-raised pork.

To his parents' puzzlement, Jun-su and Teacher Kang chatted animatedly about a village full of skeletons and underground tunnels.

After he'd left, Jun-su's mother said: "You're getting close to Teacher Kang."

Jun-su agreed that he was.

"Has he—" Jun-su's mother began a sentence, then seemed to think better of it. She glanced at her husband and began again, speaking almost in a whisper. "Has Yeong-nam ever tried to touch you?" she asked.

Jun-su was taken aback. It was also odd for his mother to refer to Teacher Kang in such an informal way. "He puts needles in me," he said, as though he didn't quite understand the question.

"Apart from when he puts the needles in you, has he ever touched you?"

Jun-su noticed his parents exchanging another glance. He knew the answer was yes.

"The thing is, he's not a normal fellow," said Jun-su's father, who was sitting cross-legged on the floor polishing his work shoes for the next day. In between polishes, he'd hold them up to the bulb to assess the shine. "Too much time studying books has given him crazy ideas. It's made him—" So-dok hesitated. Han-na had caught his eye with a warning look. "Your mother just wants to know that he hasn't done anything he shouldn't have. We wouldn't blame you if he had."

Jun-su knew that if he told his parents a word of what had happened, that would spell the end of the game.

"No," he said. "He never did."

* * *

The underground tunnels turned out to be the hiding place for the priests of a sinister cult who had conjured the skeletons to life from the graves around the village. At one point, Bong Chon-ju was surprised by so many opponents that Jun-su panicked and couldn't decide what to do first. Should he attack the lead skeleton or prepare a spell? Try to escape or stay and fight?

"What is taking you so long?" asked Teacher Kang.

"I'm trying to think what's best," said Jun-su. Sententiously, he added: "The Great Leader says the best course of action is clear to the man who is practical."

Teacher Kang gave a sly smile as he poured the yut sticks from one cupped hand to another. "Really," he said, "is this any time to be practical?"

It took almost two weeks of regular sessions to defeat the cult and for Bong Chon-ju to return in glory to the tavern and tell the villagers that they could go back to their homes.

Out of gratitude, they gave Bong Chon-ju not only the one hundred gold pieces they'd promised as payment, but a magic shirt that protected him from fire and a spell book with two new spells in it: "Speak with Animals" and "Detect Treasure."

Jun-su was giddy with excitement as he walked the old man to the door. He asked if one day he could be the game leader and throw the yut sticks. Teacher Kang said he could, and he promised to lend him a dictionary so he could try to read the book himself.

"In any case," said Teacher Kang, "the needles have done their work. You'll be well enough to return to school in January."

Jun-su detected a note of regret in the teacher's voice.

By New Year, Jun-su's shaking had all but stopped. He was sometimes breathless when he climbed stairs, but he'd put on weight and looked well. By contrast, he was shocked to see how thin his classmates had become in his absence. There were many empty spaces in the classroom that belonged to boys who had been taken out of school. Now and again, Jun-su would hear his mother say she had seen some of them begging for food around the markets.

On his first day back, at midmorning, all the students were given a protein supplement sent by their comrades in China that they mixed with water and drank. It tasted like sawdust, but the teachers insisted they finish every drop. Jun-su's friend Sok-chung informed him that this was now a daily occurrence.

A few days after Jun-su got back to school, Teacher Kang called him to stay behind after a math lesson. Teacher Kang was marking a test. He worked his way through the pile of exercise books without looking at Jun-su.

"Do you feel better?" said Teacher Kang, keeping his gaze fixed on the column of sums in front of him.

"Yes, Teacher Kang," said Jun-su.

"Good. I want you to work hard. You've missed a lot of lessons."

Jun-su agreed that he had and promised that he would do his best.

Teacher Kang closed the book he was marking and added it to the pile, which he squared up on the desk in front of him, then cleared his throat. Now he looked Jun-su in the eye. He let his gaze rest on the boy for an uncomfortably long time. Finally he spoke. "The House of Possibility is not something that everyone can understand," he said quietly.

Jun-su felt obliged to lower his eyes.

"A wise adventurer knows when to be silent," added Teacher Kang.

"Yes, Teacher Kang," said Jun-su.

The teacher dismissed him with a nod.

Jun-su and Teacher Kang resumed their old relationship, the relationship of pupil and teacher, which in Korean culture is marked with respect and great formality. But even though, outwardly, Jun-su had returned to normal life, he knew that his long absence and protracted isolation had altered him.

He found himself at one remove from his surroundings. At moments during his busy days he would fall into a reverie in which the world summoned by the words of Teacher Kang and the click of the yut sticks seemed more real than the world in front of his eyes: the red-kerchiefed students, the pedestrians in the streets of Wonsan, the smell of polish in the hallway of his apartment block.

As he stood in line in the playground before class, Jun-su thought about the sorcerer Bong Chon-ju. He imagined him mixing potions or studying magic in a tower somewhere, far from Wonsan. Jun-su wondered about his life. When he wasn't adventuring, what sorts of things did he do? Did he eat corn porridge for breakfast? Did he attend weekly self-criticism sessions of the Magicians' Union? Were there portraits of the Dear and Great Leaders in the room where he studied magic? And sometimes, when Jun-su raised his hand in class to answer a question, he even pretended that he was Bong Chon-ju himself, gathering a ball of light with his fingers to cast a spell over his classmates.

In the middle of February, the school celebrated the Dear Leader's birthday. Every child was given an egg to mark the occasion. Jun-su carried his home carefully in the palm of his hand.

Winter eased its grip on Wonsan. The silence of the ice-locked city gave way to the noisy dripping of thaw and slush. The weather grew warmer. In April, Jun-su and his entire class were sent to the countryside to plant rice. The journey took twelve hours and required a change of trains and a long walk from the station at the other end. The students brought with them not only a change of clothes but a supply of food for the length of the two-week stay.

The work was hard. The children had to transplant rice seedlings from the nursery to the paddy field by hand. It meant bending double for most of the day, and the tiny plants had to be handled delicately.

As he fixed the pale-green seedlings in the mud, Jun-su would let his thoughts wander to the game he had played with Teacher Kang. Instead of his parents' apartment, the clatter of the yut sticks, and the smell of food wafting from the kitchen, he recalled it as if he were Bong Chon-ju himself, pressed against the sides of the underground tunnels and holding his breath so he wouldn't be noticed by the cult's defenders. His nostrils were full of the smell of damp earth and the oily smoke of the torches that lit the darkness. He could hear the distant, gruff voices of the guards and the sound of his heart, beating in his chest.

Something bright was shining in his eyes. A face he didn't recognize was leaning over him. Jun-su felt wetness under his head. He was lying down in the paddy field. Two of his classmates helped him sit up.

Around him there was a babble of concerned voices. Jun-su was confused. He couldn't understand anything they were saying.

A moment later, he was sitting on a low cot in a hut while the collective farm's medical officer pressed a stethoscope to his chest.

"Your classmates said you were ill last autumn for a long time," said the medical officer. She was wearing a white coat adorned with one of the newest and most desirable badges: a joint portrait of the Dear Leader and the Great Leader.

"I had rhythmatic fever," said Jun-su.

"Rhythmatic, you say?" On the wall behind the medical officer was a picture of a human body with all its skin taken off. Labels pointed out the names of the different muscles. "Or might it have been *rheumatic* fever?"

"That's right," said Jun-su. "Rheumatic fever. And a shaking illness."

The medical officer nodded. She had a distant look in her eyes as she listened to the stethoscope and pressed its bell onto the front and back of his chest. The metal felt smooth and cool against his skin.

"Did you take medicine?" she asked. "Any antibiotics?"

Jun-su shook his head. "Teacher Kang used needles on me." Jun-su experienced a pang as he said the name of his teacher. He felt lonely in the strange hut. He wished he were back at home with his mother, reading *The Amazing Tincture* for the hundredth time and watching the sunlight advance across the wall of the room. "What can you hear?" he asked.

The medical officer put away her stethoscope in a little case. Jun-su could see Chinese characters on it. "Do you know what kind of sound the heart makes?" she said.

"It goes *boom-boom*, like a drum," said Jun-su.

"That's right," said the medical officer. "But sometimes, when I listen to your heart through the stethoscope, I hear a whooshing sound after the *boom-boom*."

"Is that bad?" said Jun-su.

The medical officer went to the corner of the room and washed her hands with water from a jug. She dried them on a small towel and then came back and sat on the end of Jun-su's cot. She pushed her hair away from her face and sighed. There was something dainty and birdlike in her movements. After a long while, she spoke.

"The illness you had can last a long time and sometimes it can damage the valves in your heart," she said.

Jun-su's face must have betrayed how ominous this all sounded to him.

She ruffled his hair. "Don't worry. It just means you need to rest. You can't work in the fields. We'll have to find some other things for you to do. I studied in Wonsan and I have a friend at the hospital who can examine you properly when you go home."

For the remainder of the stay in the countryside, Jun-su helped in the farm's small noodle factory. Sometimes he collected eggs from the henhouses. These were distributed to the workers at the collective farm. The schoolchildren ate the food rations they'd brought with them from the city.

One mealtime, a classmate called Ryu Bong-li jeered at Jun-su because he no longer worked with the others in the paddy field. "Jun-su does little girls' work," said Bong-li.

Without a moment's hesitation, Jun-su snapped back, "Bong-li is a moron. And his father wears women's clothes and dances for sailors."

Jun-su wasn't sure what had suggested the insult. It had arisen spontaneously from some secret part of him. But it hit its target like a Magic Arrow spell. The other boys laughed uproariously. Bong-li flushed with shame. His eyes went glassy and he lowered his head to hide his tears.

No one mocked Jun-su again. Sometimes when he had finished his chores, he helped the medical officer in her hut. Her name was Park Ok-ja. Jun-su called her Dr. Park.

Dr. Park weighed all her patients and let Jun-su write down their weights in a big hardback book. She also showed him how to take their blood pressure. Regardless of the patient's symptoms, the treatment was almost always the same: a screw of gray paper with some tablets in it. The doctor said they were made from willow bark and effective for many different things. She also had some dried milk powder in a big tin that she gave to nursing mothers.

Occasionally grateful patients made small presents of food to the doctor: some rice cakes, dried fruit—even once a small pot of honey from a pregnant woman who had been trying a long time to conceive. The doctor would make an effort to refuse the gifts, but without success. On quiet afternoons, she shared these with Jun-su. She also let him play with the medical equipment, such as it was. Jun-su liked pumping up the rubber sleeve for taking blood pressure on his biceps until his fingers went fat and numb.

At other times, Dr. Park would sit on the cot and Jun-su would tell her the stories from comic books. Often she seemed distracted or uninterested. But when he told her *The Blizzard in the Jungle* he made the central character a heroic female doctor, and he could tell she liked that one.

On the last day, as the children assembled to march off to the railway station for the twelve-hour journey home, Dr. Park came to say good-bye to Jun-su. She gave him a letter to take to her friend at Wonsan Hospital. In return, he gave her a small bunch of flowers that he had picked that morning and had clutched in his sweaty hand despite the teasing of his classmates. She took the flowers, kissed him on the cheek, and called him her younger brother.

It was midnight when they reached Wonsan. The students were told that, owing to their late arrival, they could come to school at midday.

Jun-su slept unusually deeply that night. He had a dream that he was back in the medical hut with Dr. Park.

She was pressing the stethoscope to his chest and listening. As she moved the bell of the stethoscope down his sternum, he could feel her warm breath tickling his skin. Dr. Park removed the earpieces and laid her hand on his stomach. "Would you like me to touch your pepper?" she asked.

Jun-su realized that the answer was *yes*, very much *yes*; but he was also worried that it was a trap.

Dr. Park seemed to read his mind. "I won't tell the *bowibu*," she whispered. "Also it will increase your vital energy."

As Jun-su considered his reply, there was a banging on the door of the hut.

"Quickly," said Dr. Park. "Someone's coming. What's your answer?"

Tormented by his desire and yet too timid to acknowledge it, Jun-su felt himself being pried out of the dream by the noise. He longed to go back and say *yes*, but now he found that he was at home in the flat in Wonsan, his dirty clothes in a heap at the foot of the mattress. It was midmorning. His father was at work. His mother had gone out.

The sound of the banging continued from the front door.

Jun-su opened it to find Kim Song-hwa, the superintendent of the building's People's Unit, chiding him from the threshold. Her thin mop of dyed black hair was teased up around her head like a lampshade. "What are you doing?" she snapped.

"Nothing," said Jun-su, still feeling oddly guilty about his dream.

"Exactly," said Mrs. Kim. "And you're supposed to be at school."

"Not this morning, Superintendent Kim. We got back late from the countryside."

"Nonsense," said Mrs. Kim, waving an official-looking piece of paper at him. "Special order. Hurry, or I'll have to put your name in the book."

The book she was referring to was the ledger in which she recorded all the shortcomings of the building's residents. It meant there would be repercussions at the next Women's Union self-criticism session and his mother would probably be reprimanded and made to paint something or sweep ash from the building's boiler room. There was no point arguing.

"I'll get dressed now, Superintendent Kim," said Jun-su.

Naturally, there was no one at the assembly point and Jun-su didn't hurry on his way. He strolled towards the school, knowing they weren't expecting him until after lunch.

*Lunch.* His parents had left the apartment early and he hadn't had time to have breakfast. Now he wouldn't eat until evening. Just then, Jun-su's nostrils were assailed by the aroma of frying food. It brought a flood of saliva into his mouth. At a cart whose misshapen wheels were propped against a couple of bricks, a vendor was frying maize flour into crispy balls. Heated from below by twigs and charcoal, the golden fat seethed in the fryer. Jun-su wondered how the man had come by so much precious oil.

A handful of pedestrians had stopped to watch, as though they might satisfy their hunger by consuming the food with their eyes.

Jun-su had no money, but he drew closer all the same. The man was working quickly, fishing out the finished balls and putting them in a cone of newspaper. Undoubtedly, he would have carefully removed any references to the Dear Leader, so as not to desecrate his name or image with hot fat.

The vendor looked a bit shifty. He kept glancing around; whether it was for customers or police, it was hard to say.

The Arduous March meant that the authorities turned a blind eye to men and women who had set up small businesses like this one, yet they weren't officially permitted. People called them "grasshopper traders," because they popped up out of nowhere and then disappeared as quickly as they'd come. It was difficult to know whether they were good or bad. On one hand, you could say they were feeding their fellow citizens and demonstrating their own version of Juche. On the other hand, any private enterprise was a small step towards re-creating the evils of capitalism and the exploitation of one class by another.

The vendor glanced at Jun-su and beckoned him forward with a nod of his head. Jun-su approached the cart and unthinkingly received the greasy paper cone that was placed in his hand.

"I don't have any money," protested Jun-su feebly.

"It's your lucky day," said the vendor.

Scarcely believing his good fortune, Jun-su put one of the snacks in his mouth: the crispy maize was splattered with spicy red gochujang sauce. At that moment, it seemed like the most delicious thing he'd ever eaten in his life.

Seeing Jun-su crunching the hot maize balls was too much

for the wavering bystanders. First two and then three others stepped forward to hand over money for the snacks.

The vendor winked at Jun-su. It seemed as though the two of them had performed a trick that had unlocked the money of the other customers. Jun-su hung around briefly in case the vendor felt like giving him more, but it wasn't to be.

He couldn't wait to get to school to share the story of his good luck with his classmates. But as he rounded the final corner to approach the school, he was taken aback to see a huge crowd of people milling around the gates.

Soldiers in khaki uniforms were pushing the crowd back and making them form an orderly queue. One of the soldiers spotted Jun-su. "Let the children in first!" he shouted.

Jun-su was ushered to the front and slipped into the school playground, which was packed with people.

He joined his classmates inside the square that marked the air raid assembly point and found himself next to Sok-chung. He couldn't help feeling excited. Had the Yankees finally attacked? Was this the moment of destiny that the entire country had been preparing for?

"What's going on?" he whispered to Sok-chung.

Sok-chung shook his head. "I'm not sure, but I think it's a special visit."

Jun-su suddenly knew exactly what was happening. He knew the reason for the crowds, the sense of excitement—and even, in a strange way, for his good fortune with the food vendor.

In a few minutes, the gates would open and a car would arrive bearing the Dear Leader, Kim Jong-il. The Dear Leader loved Wonsan. It was rumored that he had a home somewhere along the coast. He'd definitely visited the Songdowon Hotel with his father in 1972, because the moment was commemorated by a mural in the lobby.

Now he was about to turn up at Jun-su's school and give some on-the-spot guidance. He would congratulate the students on their hard work in the countryside. He might even single out individuals for praise. Jun-su felt a pang of misgiving that he hadn't spent more time laboring in the fields. He hoped the Dear Leader would understand that his health problems had made it impossible.

Just as Jun-su had predicted, the crowd parted, and two vehicles began to nose slowly through the mass of people.

It took an age for them to reach the space that had been cleared at the front of the playground. They had to move carefully so as not to crush anyone.

Jun-su could hear shouts from the soldiers and now a woman's voice, yelling above the murmur of the crowd. She sounded hysterical. Some people's love for the Dear Leader was so intense that it spilled out in passionate declarations like this. Except this didn't sound quite right.

The woman was pounding on the door of one of the vehicles and screaming, "Bastard! Bastard!"

A soldier had to pull her back, but he didn't arrest her.

Jun-su looked in puzzlement at Sok-chung.

"Tae-il's mother," said Sok-chung. Seo Tae-il was the class representative who had visited Jun-su when he had first fallen ill. Tae-il's father was high up in the Workers' Party and the boy had already been accepted into the Young Pioneers, the first in their class to receive this honor.

Now Jun-su started to notice other strange preparations for the visit. A layer of sand had been raked over the concrete in front of them. The two vehicles were green army jeeps, not the luxury cars that the Dear Leader would travel in.

Soldiers dismounted from one of the jeeps and pulled a heavy sack out of the other one. They dumped it on the sand in front of the crowd.

One of the soldiers kicked the sack and it stood up and turned into a person: a pair of legs in stained trousers, a filthy torso, hands manacled tightly behind its back, head and shoulders covered with a loose black hood.

It took a couple of uncertain steps, like someone who had been spun around a lot with his eyes closed.

A soldier with a rough voice read loudly from a piece of paper. "Kang Yeong-nam, the people's court finds you guilty of spying. The sentence is death."

As the old teacher tottered on his thin and unsteady legs, three soldiers stepped forward and discharged their weapons three times each with loud cracks. Three shots went into Yeong-nam's head, three into his body, and three into the backs of his knees. He crumpled onto the sand. The silence seemed thicker after the gunshots. Blood puddled around the black sack.

The bittersweet, wet-iron smell of butchery rose up to Jun-su's nose. He could feel the greasy maize balls in his stomach like stones. He thought of his teeth breaking through their crunchy shells and the sickly red chili paste. He felt sure he was going to vomit. He turned round and pushed his way through the silent crowd.

By the time he'd got outside, he no longer felt sick. But he wanted to cry, and he didn't want anyone to see his tears.

Over the coming days, the teacher's execution was all that anyone talked about. People remembered many wicked things that Kang Yeong-nam had done—no one now considered him worthy of the honorific *Teacher*. Sometimes, as people competed to reveal his crimes, Jun-su thought about sharing his own story of the teacher's depravity. But something held him back—some guilt at not having spoken out, some questionable sense of loyalty, some residual affection for the old man.

The spurious tales of Kang Yeong-nam's wickedness supplanted other, accurate recollections about his generosity and devotion to teaching.

It turned out that his disloyalty had finally been exposed thanks to the vigilance of Seo Tae-il, the class representative, who had been receiving extra math lessons from the old man.

The story went that Seo Tae-il had discovered a secret radio in Kang Yeong-nam's apartment that he used to communicate with foreign spies.

Seo Tae-il had revealed this to his father. Under questioning, the teacher had admitted to many other terrible crimes. The death sentence was undoubtedly just. Seo Tae-il received a special commendation from the party and his status in the school rose to previously inconceivable heights. There was even an article about him in the *Rodong Sinmun*.

Armed with the letter from Dr. Park, Jun-su was able to get an appointment at the hospital in Wonsan.

Dr. Park's friend was the head of the pediatric department. He was a bony man in his forties called Dr. Ri who smoked the same Chollima brand of cigarettes as Jun-su's dad. Han-na had brought him a gift of food. He accepted it wordlessly, but closed his eyes and nodded in a way that left no doubt about how welcome it was.

The checkup confirmed Dr. Park's suspicions that Jun-su's illness had damaged his heart. There was, however, little the hospital could do. As a precaution, the doctor advised that Jun-su should not participate in sports or any strenuous outdoor pursuits.

This was crushing for Jun-su. When his classmates were given days off to help in the collective farm, Jun-su did extra schoolwork. During gymnastics and soccer or volleyball practice, Jun-su swept the changing room and cleaned the showers. After his classmates finished showering, Jun-su mopped up the puddles on the floor with a bundle of rags on a pole. He hated the drudgery and he envied the carefree athleticism of the other boys, whose skinny bodies were now beginning to show the changes of puberty.

One afternoon at the end of volleyball practice, Jun-su found himself alone in the showers with Tae-il. Tae-il, despite not being particularly good at volleyball, was on the school team. Better still, as a reward for his vigilance in exposing Kang Yeong-nam, he had received a gift of almost unimaginable marvelousness: a red nylon tracksuit like the ones worn by the country's Olympic athletes.

Tae-il zipped up the jacket with an air of self-importance while Jun-su waited with his tatty mop.

A thought struck Jun-su as he watched Tae-il flattening out his bangs in front of the mirror.

"Hey, Tae-il," he said. "You know when the traitor Kang was teaching you math?"

Tae-il inclined his head casually to Jun-su. He was fond of retelling the story on which his legendary status depended. And in truth, both the danger he'd faced and his resourcefulness had increased in subsequent tellings.

Jun-su went on: "Did you two ever play the House of Possibility?"

Tae-il's face suddenly altered. His features now wore an expression that Jun-su had never seen. He looked alert and fearful. His newly prominent Adam's apple bobbed twice in his throat as he swallowed. He glanced around to check that they were alone.

Jun-su moved towards him. He was astonished by the shifty expression on Tae-il's face: a look of guilt and discomfort.

He thought of Teacher Kang trying to touch his pepper and he knew instantly he'd done the same to Tae-il. "Teacher Kang touched you," he said, uttering the words almost inadvertently, just as they had crossed his mind.

Tae-il's face flushed and he began to shout; his rasping, broken voice sounded like a panicky quack. "Jun-su is a spy!" he yelled.

The years of political study, of math problems that involved multiplying numbers of American soldiers by numbers of missiles, of learning the history of the Korean Workers' Party and the exemplary life stories of the Dear and Great Leaders meant that Jun-su knew immediately what Tae-il was doing. He wasn't just reacting defensively with his counteraccusation. He was attempting to lay on Jun-su an irreversible and fatal curse. Any hesitation now would be calamitous.

Jun-su instantly drew his arm back and gave Tae-il's face a ringing slap.

Tae-il was stunned into silence by the decisiveness of the movement. The handle of Jun-su's mop clattered onto the floor.

"I know exactly what you did with Teacher Kang," said Jun-su. "You chose to be evil and you let him touch your cock."

Tae-il stared at him disbelievingly, clutching his face. His eyes burned with shame and hatred.

At that moment, the door of the changing room opened. Teacher Kim, their form mistress, called for the boys to hurry up. Jun-su knew she wouldn't come into the boys' room unless it was an emergency. He stood his ground, not taking his eyes off Tae-il.

"Coming, Teacher Kim!" quacked Tae-il, and he skulked out of the changing room, leaving Jun-su to pick up the mop.

# THE YOUNG LOVERS

On his twelfth birthday, Jun-su received a badge of the Great Leader that he would from now on wear at all times over his heart.

It was a symbol of his passage into adulthood and his devotion to the ideals of the Democratic People's Republic. It should have been a moment of celebration, but Jun-su was aware that his ill-health had cast a shadow over him.

His infirmity meant he was shut out of the group activities that bonded the students to each other and allowed them to demonstrate their loyalty to the regime.

Mindful that he was being cast in the role of a sickly outsider, and perhaps aware of the dangers that it might bring, Jun-su became extra zealous to fit in.

He cheered his classmates from the touchline when they played soccer or volleyball against other schools. His voice was the loudest when they sang revolutionary songs. In his free time, he organized petitions against Yankee imperialism. Most of all, he found that he had a knack for writing patriotic poetry, which he was encouraged to read aloud at school assemblies. As the years passed, his compositions were met with increasing success.

At the end of 1998, Jun-su wrote a long poem about Mount Paektu that was awarded first prize in a regional poetry competition. It was a conventional subject for loyal bards: Paektu was the sacred mountain in the north of the country on top of which the Dear Leader had been born in 1942 on February 16, the Day of the Shining Star.

The contest had been held nationwide, and in the spring of 1999 the regional winners were all invited to the capital to read their poems at a special event where, rumor had it, the Dear Leader himself might be present.

It was a tremendous honor. In the company of a young teacher, Mun Byung-gak, Jun-su traveled to the capital.

Teacher Mun and Jun-su left Wonsan at five o'clock in the morning. Teacher Mun, who had also been given a small per diem for their expenses, was overcome with excitement as they boarded the first bus. It was the first time either of them had been to Pyongyang—the greatest and most advanced city on earth.

* * *

By now, the Arduous March had just passed its height. Bus and train schedules were still in chaos, but the Regional Party Committee had given Teacher Mun a special letter that had an extraordinary effect on anyone he showed it to. It explained that all reasonable assistance should be rendered to the bearers, whose presence was urgently required in the capital.

The formal language, the letterhead, and the officious way Teacher Mun flourished it produced astonishing reactions from recalcitrant truck drivers, bus drivers, and even a snack-bar attendant at Sin Pyong Lake, who not only fed them but insisted that both Jun-su and Teacher Mun honor him by reciting some verses and drinking a glass of snake wine.

Fourteen hours after setting off, they arrived at the university hostel in Pyongyang where the regional winners were billeted.

Jun-su was by now almost sixteen. He was tall and, unlike many of his classmates, showed no outward signs of malnourishment. He had an alert, sensitive face and had developed a sharp sense of humor, which he often deployed to charm and less often to ward off would-be bullies.

The reception for the competition winners was held in the foyer of the library at Kim Il-sung University. Everyone wore name-cards. There were seventy or eighty people, Jun-su guessed. After the speeches, the attendees milled around and made small talk. There was beer for the adult men and soft drinks for the women and children. Jun-su was approached by a pretty girl of about his age. She wore a pair of wire-framed glasses that emphasized the pleasing symmetry of her plump face. She also had on a pleated blue skirt, a white blouse, and the red neckerchief they all wore.

"I enjoyed your verses, comrade," she said. All the short-listed poems had been printed in the Kim Il-sung Socialist Youth League's monthly magazine.

Jun-su bowed graciously and told her she was very kind.

"Who are your influences?" she asked.

"I would have to choose Oh Young-jae," said Jun-su, naming the country's poet laureate, who had recently been declared a Labor Hero.

"Comrade Oh is a writer of superlative talent," said the girl, somehow giving the impression that she knew him personally. "Which of his poems do you like the most?"

There was a challenge in the way she put the question. It was almost as if she was testing him. Her radiant good health, foreign-made glasses, and air of confidence marked her out as a member of the elite. Jun-su was keenly aware of the disparity in their status: he was, after all, a bumpkin from a suburb of Wonsan whose mother kept pigs in a lean-to. A few of the other finalists and their chaperones had drawn closer to eavesdrop on their conversation.

"My favorite?" said Jun-su. "So many good ones, so hard to choose." He narrowed his eyes and looked up to the corner of the room.

"You must have one," said the girl. Some of the bystanders were starting to enjoy Jun-su's apparent discomfort. Also, to anyone with half a brain the answer was obvious: Oh Young-jae's masterpiece *Taedong River*, about the construction of the West Sea Dam, was a six-thousand-line epic, the longest poem written in Korean.

Jun-su waited as long as possible. He wanted his audience to think that his mind was a blank. At the moment of maximum awkwardness he cleared his throat and addressed the young woman directly. Jun-su's voice was low and pleasing and he recited well: "'Ah, your bosom is a bosom that blooms, and embroiders our leader's great will into the earth! You are a clear, firm, and sparkling crystal egg, raised by our socialist fatherland.'"

There was a murmur of appreciation for Jun-su's recall of this early poem of Oh's, "The Girl Loved by the Fatherland."

The girl blushed and her lips parted with pleasure, revealing pearly white teeth. "Bravo, comrade," she said. Her name was Ri Su-ok.

After a special breakfast in the cafeteria that included eggs and fine white rice, the winners of the poetry competition spent the following day sightseeing in the capital. Ri Su-ok joined them, though she was a resident of Pyongyang and already knew its landmarks well. She and her teacher sat alongside Jun-su and Teacher Mun in the bus.

Out of the window, Jun-su saw men in khaki crouched by the water's edge. "The soldiers are washing their clothes in the Taedong River," said Jun-su. "Does Oh Young-jae write about that?"

"They are very resourceful," said Su-ok. "Are you looking forward to military service, comrade?"

This was a painful subject. Jun-su didn't want to admit to having health problems that ruled him out of being in the People's Army, so he said he was.

The sophistication and smartness of the capital were intoxicating. Teacher Mun had borrowed a tiny Chinese-made camera, but it only had one roll of film with twenty-four exposures. He was tormented about when to use them. He had already used up two taking pictures of their breakfast and could have happily shot the rest of the roll at Mangyondae, the Great Leader's ancestral village and birthplace. In the end, he hit on the plan of rationing himself to one an hour. By the time the coach parked outside the Mansudae Theater for the final readings, he only had four left.

Lights had been set up in the auditorium by a camera crew from state television, who were recording the readings for broadcast at some future date. The heat and glare from their lights made the room feel like Wonsan beach at noon in midsummer.

Backstage, the organizers lined up the competitors in their running order as the audience took their seats in the hall—the men wearing suits, the women in traditional brightly colored dresses. Su-ok and Jun-su would be the last to read. Su-ok had written her poem about Korean reunification. It had finally dawned on Jun-su that the two of them were favorites for the first prize. Previously he had told himself he didn't care if he won, but now he kept thinking how disappointed he'd feel to come second.

Half an hour before the performance was due to begin, a ripple of energy went through the auditorium. It was palpable backstage. People's movements took on a sudden urgency. Jun-su had just left his place in the lineup to get another of the fizzy blueberry drinks that had been laid out on a table for the performers. He had his back to the room and was almost the last to notice what was going on. He looked over his shoulder to ask Su-ok if she wanted a drink; he could see she was standing in front of a little man in a khaki blouson and matching trousers. She was staring straight ahead with an extraordinary fixed grin on her face.

As Jun-su attempted to retake his place in the line of poets, he found his way blocked by a burly man in a dark jacket. Jun-su protested, but it took Su-ok's intervention to let him be readmitted.

"And yours must be the poem about Mount Paektu," said the man in the khaki suit. For one of the few times in his life, Jun-su found himself utterly lost for words. He was staring into a face that he knew better than his own. It was the Dear Leader, Kim Jong-il.

Jun-su was thunderstruck. He bowed and began stammering out a long speech of thanks for everything that the Dear Leader had done for their country. An entire lifetime of political indoctrination seemed to be culminating in this moment. It was difficult to express everything he felt. Jun-su instinctively began embellishing the speech with flowery honorifics and he started tripping over his sentences. The Dear Leader—smaller, more impish, and more *human* than he'd ever been in Jun-su's imagination—waved a dismissive hand. "You honored me with a poem about my birthplace," he said. "It's enough!" The officials around him laughed at the Dear Leader's grace and good humor. Jun-su experienced a sensation of physical uplift, like the one he'd got from Teacher Kang's needles.

The Dear Leader stood between Jun-su and Su-ok for a photograph. Then he gave all the young poets a brief speech about the importance of their work in helping to form revolutionary consciousness and direct the masses.

As the Dear Leader left, Jun-su felt as though his entire body was tingling. Teacher Mun approached him with a fearful look on his face. "Forgive me, Jun-su," he whispered, holding out his hands with an object in them. It was the camera. Teacher Mun looked disconsolately at it, as though it were a small animal in its death throes. He raised it towards Jun-su. He explained that he had shot his last photograph seconds before the Dear Leader's arrival. Consequently, he had been unable to capture his encounter with Jun-su. "Forgive me," he said again in a trembling voice. But Jun-su felt immune to any disappointment. At that moment, he was sure he could have walked through fire unscathed.

The interaction with the Dear Leader had transformed the atmosphere backstage. It was as if lightning had been discharged. The air pressure had altered and the poets felt themselves crackling with new energy.

When the time came for Su-ok to read her poem, she wept actual tears as she described American soldiers who were tearing a child from the arms of its mother. This was an allegory about the division of the two Koreas—as the title of her poem, "An Allegory of Division," made clear.

Now it was Jun-su's turn to read. The host of the program, a woman in a traditional pink dress, read out his name and he walked onstage towards the lectern. It seemed to take an age for him to reach it, and as he walked he had an awful thought: What if he had a relapse of his shaking illness in front of the Dear Leader? What if his jelly legs returned now to be broadcast on national television?

He closed his eyes and gripped the sides of the lectern to steady himself. He had learned his poem by heart and began reciting it softly.

Jun-su's poem was very different from the documentary poems written by most of the other poets. Those were verses that celebrated factory work, or the construction of dams and fish farms. Jun-su's poem, however, seemed to draw on an older mythological tradition.

The Mount Paektu he described in it was full of fabulous creatures who were working to safeguard the Dear Leader and the Korean people. Some were mining precious jewels. Some were creating weapons with incredible powers to protect the country from invasion. It was a strange and evocative poem. Its message seemed to be that, despite all the forces ranged against it, the North Korean people's destiny would be protected by mythical beings from the country's distant past. The Mount Paektu of the poem was a strange semireligious blend of Mount Sinai, Mount Olympus, and the fantastic worlds of Wagner or Tolkien—names, of course, unknown to Jun-su or his audience. It was a brave, stirring, and unusual vision. Before he was halfway through, Jun-su knew he had won the competition.

The announcement of his victory was followed by deafening applause. Su-ok was the first to congratulate him.

Jun-su thanked her and respectfully congratulated her on her poem in return.

"There's something special about your verses, comrade," said Su-ok.

Jun-su demurred and said she was very kind. But of course, he knew exactly what it was that made his verses special. It was the House of Possibility.

After Teacher Kang's death, months had passed before Jun-su felt able to open the mysterious book and think about the

House of Possibility. When he did, he was amazed to see what Teacher Kang had done to it. The book's printed paragraphs were spaced widely apart. The white expanses between them had been filled up with delicately penciled annotations. The teacher had parsed the most complicated English words with *chosongul* equivalents. It must have been an immense labor. Jun-su flipped through the pages. *Wooden club*, he read. *Frost giant. Elemental evil. Crusading knight. Singing warrior. Love potion.* It was so lovingly and clearly done. Through the jungle of words, a narrow, almost imperceptible path seemed to beckon towards an unknown destination.

For two years, Jun-su had spent his spare hours working his way through the book. In one way, fate had been kind to him. A previous generation of North Korean students had learned Russian and Chinese as a matter of course. Since the Arduous March, English was taught in an increasing number of schools—Jun-su's included. "Foreign Language Study Is a Weapon for Life and Struggle," said a new slogan. Knowing that the English language was the key that would unlock the House of Possibility motivated Jun-su to study hard.

The teaching in his school, however, was not of a high standard. Teacher Mun's command of the language was poor. The second year of study consisted of going through *The Ragged Trousered Philanthropists* by Robert Tressell word by word, in old Soviet editions that had footnotes in Russian. It was grim, painstaking work, but good preparation for the task that faced Jun-su.

Jun-su understood he needed an English dictionary and began pestering his parents to buy him one. They weren't easy to get hold of. Fortunately, one place where they were occasionally available was in the bookshop at the Songdowon Hotel. So-dok had a word with the woman who ran the shop, and when a new consignment of stock was delivered she put a copy aside for him. So-dok took Jun-su with him when he went to pay for it. It was an enormous red tome, thousands of pages long, entitled *New Korean English Dictionary*. "How much?" asked So-dok.

"Three hundred won," said the bookseller.

So-dok looked in discomfort at the book. The price was six times his monthly salary at the time. "It's so heavy," he said, weighing the volume in his hand. "I don't think he'll be able to use it."

Instead, So-dok paid ten won for the *English–Korean Word Book*, a pamphlet of fewer than fifty pages intended for foreign tourists that included such phrases as: "I don't eat pork. I'll have chicken or pheasant"; "Such a miracle could only occur in North Korea"; and "Let us mutilate US imperialism."

"How is it?" he said brightly to Jun-su. Jun-su thanked his father. He was careful not to seem ungrateful, but the book was essentially useless.

Instead, Jun-su decided to use the dictionaries in the Foreign Language section of Wonsan Library. It was such a popular place to study that you needed to reserve a slot in advance.

The first time Jun-su went there, he took the book wrapped in its brown paper cover. Translating was hard work. As fast as he looked up the words, they disappeared from his mind. Things were complicated further by the fact that Korean and English word order is completely different. By the time he'd got to the end of a sentence, he no longer remembered what the words at the beginning of it meant. Jun-su realized that he'd have to write down his translations in order to make sense of the book. But then another problem arose.

On his third or fourth visit, the female librarian came over to see what he was reading.

The students in the carrels alongside him were doing computing. In the absence of actual computer terminals, they were practicing their typing skills on keyboards made from paper and writing out the commands of their programs longhand.

"What are you working on, comrade?" asked the woman with a friendly smile.

"It's a school assignment," said Jun-su, improvising hastily. "I'm translating this book."

"Is it a foreign book, comrade?" The librarian had a clear, bell-like voice that cut through the hush of the library.

"Yes," said Jun-su, immediately realizing that this was the wrong answer. "What I mean is, technically it's a foreign book. But it was published by our fraternal socialist allies."

"Which ones, comrade?"

Which ones? Jun-su swallowed. As much as he trusted his

quick wits, he sensed a void beginning to open beneath him. He was lying through his teeth, but he was too far in to stop now.

"The Cubans," he said.

This brazen answer bought him a bit of time. It was unclear what the official party line on Cuban literature was at the moment. The librarian didn't seem sure. But the plucky resistance of the Cubans to Yankee imperialism was celebrated annually at the Mass Games by North Korean dancers in straw hats and blackface.

Jun-su knew that if the librarian asked to examine the book, flipped through it, or—worse still—looked at the image concealed beneath the brown cover, the consequences would be devastating. People went to prison for much less. He had to retain the initiative—and pray that she didn't speak English.

"It's a fascinating book, comrade," he said. "It's a book published by the Cuban Workers' Party about the mathematics of probability." He pushed the book's open pages towards the librarian. "See? It shows methods to calculate the probability of all kinds of events with these charts."

At the mention of the word *mathematics*, the librarian visibly relaxed: it was a relatively uncontroversial subject. "Aha!" she said, glancing down at the dense pages containing the rules for melee combat. "It's in Spanish!"

"That's right," lied Jun-su, smiling and nodding. This time the librarian was satisfied, but Jun-su knew he could never risk bringing the book again.

From then on, he copied out pages from the book which he inserted into his schoolwork. Using the library's dictionaries, he made rough translations of these pages into a series of exercise books.

Helped by the legacy of Teacher Kang's annotations, Jun-su gradually unpicked more and more of the mysterious book.

It yielded its secrets slowly and erratically. Some passages remained forever obscure. But bit by bit, Jun-su began to understand the nature of the game and how Teacher Kang had adapted it to make it playable.

The method Jun-su had chosen was unbelievably laborious, but given the risks it seemed the only one open to him. And it carried one unexpected advantage. The mere act of writing out long passages of the book in English began to transform his command of the language.

While his spoken English remained primitive, these private efforts gave him a fluency in reading and translation that put him leagues ahead of his classmates. And his poetry became populated with strange word choices and bizarre objects: kobolds, cuirasses, caltrops, siege towers. It was to this that Jun-su credited his success in the competition.

Shortly after the announcement of his victory, Jun-su learned that the Dear Leader had not in fact attended the readings. His time at the event had been cut short by some important matters of state. It was disappointing—as was the lack of photographs—but to Jun-su the mere fact of having been in the Dear Leader's presence and exchanging words with him was an honor he would carry with him for the rest of his life.

What's more, the change in his fortunes since their meeting was palpable. Victory in the poetry competition had shone the light of a special distinction on Jun-su and his family.

Jun-su was suddenly in demand at get-togethers of the local branch of the Workers' Party. He was invited to declaim his poem to gatherings of flushed and drunken regional officials. As he recited his verses, he would marvel at the quantity and variety of the dishes being served to the guests. Sometimes he was even given food to bring home.

On several occasions, he performed in the banqueting room at his father's hotel, and So-dok would emerge from the kitchen in his chef's whites to stand proudly at the back of the room. Han-na received orders for pork from the wives of local dignitaries, the police left her in peace, and her business, which occupied a gray area under the law, flourished.

Ordinarily, a bright provincial boy like Jun-su would be expected to attend a regional university, specialize in agriculture or engineering, and be assigned a job in the city of his birth. But as Jun-su completed his schooling and achieved outstanding grades in English and Chinese, it became clear that he was being considered for a higher calling.

Jun-su could see how much it meant to his parents. He knew what was behind it. When he saw pictures of the Dear Leader, he would mutter an inward prayer of thanks. Ever since the encounter in Pyongyang, he understood that the Dear Leader was taking a personal interest in his destiny.

In all sorts of ways, large and small, Jun-su could feel the hand of the Dear Leader smoothing the path ahead of him. So when, to almost universal astonishment, eighteen-year-old Jun-su learned that he had been accepted to study in the Department of Foreign Languages at Kim Il-sung University in Pyongyang, the only person who was not surprised was him.

On Jun-su's arrival in the capital to begin his studies at the end of August 2002, Pyongyang seemed even more magnificent than it had appeared to him as a schoolboy. Now he walked its streets with the pride of an official resident: a stamp in his internal passport authorized him to remain for the duration of his studies. The four years of his course seemed an unimaginably long time, but beyond that lay the possibility of a career in the capital, permanent residence, and the opportunity to honor his parents by making their old age comfortable and helping them to own the treasured Seven Gadgets: a sewing machine, a television, a fan, a refrigerator, a video recorder, a camera, and a washing machine.

Jun-su shared his dormitory with three other students: an engineer named Ri Song-chol; a chemist, Kim Tae-hoon; and a computer scientist called Mun Jong.

Tae-hoon and Jong were older, having already completed

their military service. Jun-su and Song-chol looked up to them. But the four students also shared certain qualities. They were all from the provinces, all thrilled to be in the city, and soon became inseparable. Song-chol christened them the Beryllium Boys, after the element with the atomic number 4.

For Jun-su, who was used to being set apart from his peers either by his disability or by his precocious career as a poet, it was a wonderful experience. Drinking alcohol was forbidden on the campus, but the older students were heavy drinkers and organized rowdy picnics outside the city center at which the four of them got drunk and pledged eternal friendship to each other.

At one of these gatherings, Jun-su told them about the House of Possibility, and they were all eager to try it out. They began playing a regular game on Sunday evenings, in which Jun-su took the role of leader. He had briefly considered bringing the actual book from home, but decided it would be imprudent. He had no real qualms about the ideological content of the game, but the cover was open to misinterpretation. So instead of the original, he brought the notebooks into which he had painstakingly copied his translations.

Until this point—and aside from the sessions with Teacher Kang—Jun-su had no actual experience of playing the game. He had never been close enough to anyone to broach the subject. He doubted his parents would be interested—and there even seemed to be something slightly indecorous about suggesting it to them.

He showed his friends how to generate the characters just as Teacher Kang had done, years earlier, using the charts and the yut sticks. He helped them name them, choose their races and professions, and he devised adventures for them to play.

It quickly became a highlight of their week. Song-chol played as Elvis the Bard; Jong was Gumiho, a barbarian fighter; and Tae-hoon commemorated Jun-su's unwitting foreign benefactor as Kapsberger, a cleric.

In the absence of the official book, Jun-su had to take a more freewheeling approach to the game. He hadn't copied out all the tables, so he used common sense and imagination when the players surprised him with courses of action that he hadn't anticipated. His players soon fell in love with the game and its odd blend of improvised drama and storytelling. In their world of politicized and state-sanctioned recreation, the House of Possibility seemed magical and liberating.

Word of this strange weekly activity spread across the campus and Jun-su was besieged with requests to join the group. He politely turned them all down. But then one day came a message that he couldn't ignore.

It was by now spring 2003. Professor Hwang, the deputy head of the computer science faculty, had heard a rumor about the unusual game being played by the Beryllium Boys. He'd asked his student Mun Jong whether it was true; Jong had confirmed that a game called the House of Possibility did in fact take place, emphasizing that it was an innocent pastime that Jun-su had devised.

Professor Hwang sent a message to Jun-su, requesting his presence at his office. There wasn't really any way around this, so one April afternoon Jun-su went to see the professor.

"Tell me about this game you play," said Professor Hwang.

Jun-su cleared his throat. He was pretty sure there was nothing wrong with playing the game, but you never knew. People were sent to prison for watching videotapes of South Korean soap operas or tuning their radios to banned foreign stations. And the roots of the game were tangled up with a dark period of his life. He'd never spoken to anyone about Teacher Kang's behavior and he wasn't sure if it was something he really understood or would ever be able to explain.

Fortunately, the professor was only interested in the technical aspects of the game. Jun-su was able to talk knowledgeably about its origins and answer the questions the professor put to him. At the end, Professor Hwang thanked him and asked if he would mind coming and giving a seminar on the same subject to some students in the computer science faculty. It was both a puzzling request and one that wasn't in Jun-su's power to refuse.

He really had no idea why elite students at Pyongyang's best university wanted to devote a seminar to learning about polyhedral dice and the relative merits of pretending to wear plate mail or chain mail, but it wasn't his place to judge.

At the professor's suggestion, on the appointed day Jun-su took Mun Jong with him so that he could give them a demonstration of the game actually being played.

The lecture hall was much more crowded than Jun-su had expected. There were sixty or so students in the audience. Professor Hwang gave a brief introduction about the game and even showed some slides of the original English-language volumes. When the *Dungeon Masters Guide* appeared on-screen with its red troll and half-naked female adventurer, there was an audible gasp followed by some nervous laughter. The decadence of the game's Yankee inventors seemed obvious. Jun-su felt suddenly anxious about the political implications of what he was about to do.

His experience performing poems had at least taught him how to conceal and sublimate his nerves. He thanked Professor Hwang and explained how the game had been invented by an American called Gary Gygax. It was essentially a codified system of make-believe that drew on archetypal myths. Jun-su ran through some of the game's mechanics, and then he and Mun Jong demonstrated the game by playing it for about ten minutes. At the end, Professor Hwang opened up the seminar to questions. Again, these were very technical—no one seemed interested in scoring political points by attacking the game or its American origins. The penultimate question came from a woman in the audience. She thanked Comrade Jun-su for his clear and informative talk and asked him to expand on the distinction between PCs and NPCs—player characters and non-player characters.

It was a straightforward question. Jun-su explained that each of the players controlled a single character: the game was about these characters, their choices, their desires, their success or failure. That's what gave the game its shape. They inhabited a world of non-player characters—essentially everyone else: innkeepers, armorers, monsters, and so forth. The non-player characters were like extras in a film. They were there so the main characters had people to interact with, kill, persuade, trade with, or learn from.

"So who plays them, comrade?" asked the woman.

"I guess I do," said Jun-su. The frankness and artlessness of what he had said struck the audience as funny. There was a ripple of good-natured laughter at his remark. And as he waited for it to die down, Jun-su realized that the woman asking the question was his old poetic rival: Ri Su-ok.

There was one more question about game mechanics; then the professor thanked Jun-su and wrapped up the talk. As Jun-su gathered up his papers, he glanced at Jong. "I still can't figure out why they want to know all this," he said, shaking his head.

Jong gave him a dismissive look. "Don't be stupid, brother," he said. "These are the hackers."

* * *

Su-ok was waiting for Jun-su outside the auditorium. "Hello, comrade," she said.

Jun-su greeted her in return. "At first I didn't recognize you without your glasses," he said. He felt strangely shy. Su-ok was much prettier than he remembered.

Now it was her turn to seem a little awkward. "I was lucky enough to have an operation to fix my eyes," she said.

"How is it possible?" asked Jun-su, genuinely puzzled.

"They can use lasers to reshape the cornea," said Su-ok.

"I've never heard of this before," said Jun-su. "The Fatherland's scientists are truly wonderful."

Su-ok looked embarrassed. "That's certainly true. But in fact, I had the operation in Beijing."

This revelation raised a number of perplexing questions that Jun-su decided it would be wise not to pursue.

"Your game sounds fascinating," Su-ok went on, clearly relieved not to be interrogated further.

"It's not really my game," said Jun-su. "For me, it's just a way to pass the time." He was aware suddenly how frivolous this sounded. "Also it teaches important values about teamwork and self-reliance. And it's been valuable for my English studies." Su-ok nodded. There was no hint of disapproval in her face. "Do you still write poetry?" Jun-su asked.

"Not anymore," she said. "I thought a lot about you after the competition, comrade. I realized the difference between being competent and having a gift."

"You're being too harsh on yourself, sister," said Jun-su.

"No. You are a true poet. I understood that I could serve the Fatherland better in other ways. My other great love, since childhood, was computing."

Jong, who was loitering nearby, coughed lightly to remind Jun-su of his presence. Jun-su introduced him. Jong bowed and then told Jun-su that he would see him back in the dormitory. As he left, he shot Jun-su a glance that was full of playful insinuations.

Jun-su walked slowly across the campus with Su-ok. She explained that since the year 2000 and the global panic over the millennium bug, it had become clear that the country's enemies were vulnerable due to their great dependence on computers.

"We are learning ways to enter and attack our enemies' computer systems," she said. "Professor Hwang is very brilliant. He understands that this is a kind of guerrilla warfare. We need to understand the people who develop these systems. They are not army people. They're *otaku*. You know what I mean? They like games like yours, comic books, playing on computers. They are people with their own culture. And we need to understand this culture to be able to understand the systems they build."

Jun-su made a deep sigh of comprehension. "Yes, I see now. That makes sense." They walked on in silence for a while. "You know," he said, "if you really want to understand this culture properly, you should come play the game."

Su-ok looked at him and tried not to smile. "That sounds like it would be instructive, comrade," she said.

From Jun-su's point of view, the evening with Su-ok was not a great success. To begin with, it had felt like a big adventure. Girls and boys were not allowed in each other's dorms, so they had to sneak Su-ok in with her hair under a cap. Jun-su had made her a character—she was a dark elf fighter called Desdemona—and he contrived a bit of backstory so she could join the adventure in the middle. But when the game started, his three roommates were awkward in her presence. Their self-consciousness made it harder to fall into character and their interactions lacked the spontaneity that made the game fun. Towards the end, Song-chol fell into a sulk when his character got injured by a trap that he had failed to find.

It was eight o'clock when they stopped playing and Jun-su walked Su-ok to her trolleybus stop: since she was a Pyongyang native, she lived off-campus with her parents.

Rain was falling as they emerged from the dormitory, so Jun-su asked Su-ok to wait while he ran back to get an umbrella.

He climbed the stairs two at a time, barged in, grabbed his umbrella breathlessly, and took the opportunity to yell at his friends. "You behaved like dicks," he said. "What's so hard about being polite?"

"Don't be self-conscious, brother. She had a good time," said Jong, looking up from his notebooks.

"I couldn't concentrate because she's too beautiful," said Song-chol.

Jun-su threw a chemistry textbook at his head. Song-chol laughed as the book flopped onto the floor.

The exertion had made his heart pound and Jun-su was quite out of breath when he got back to Su-ok, who was waiting on the path. He held the umbrella over her head. There were rolling blackouts in the capital and the night enveloped them in its darkness. It took a while for Jun-su's eyes to get used to it again.

"You're not fit, comrade!" she teased him. "You need to do some physical training."

Su-ok must have seen a shadow pass over Jun-su's face. His poor constitution was a matter of great shame to him.

Near the trolleybus stop stood a cigarette kiosk. Students were forbidden to smoke, but the kiosk also sold sweets and occasionally ice cream. Its owner was lighting a candle in the window.

"Blueberry jellies!" said Su-ok, pointing at a box in the kiosk display.

Jun-su asked Su-ok to hold the umbrella and he reached into his pocket for his money. He paid for the sweets and gave them to her with a flourish. "A memento of this evening," he said. "And also of our first meeting."

Su-ok accepted them graciously and she knew very well what he meant. According to the label, the sweets were made from Mount Paektu blueberries, and Jun-su was alluding to their first encounter at the poetry competition, where fizzy blueberry drinks had been served.

"I'm glad we met again, Jun-su," she said as they set off, using his name for the first time he could remember.

"I hope the game was useful. It wasn't the best session. Song-chol was in a funny mood."

"Apart from the game, it's nice to see you. I thought about you a lot after the competition."

It seemed too much to hope that she meant something by this.

"You're from Wonsan, aren't you?" said Su-ok.

Jun-su nodded.

"I love Wonsan. It has the best beaches in the world. Better even than Spain."

"You've been to China *and* Spain?" asked Jun-su incredulously.

"My father is a diplomat," said Su-ok. "I lived in Spain until I was ten."

Jun-su had a thousand questions. To live overseas was an unimaginable privilege. To be a diplomat was a dream so marvelous that he dared not admit it to himself. He wanted to know how that was possible. And he wanted to know what Spain was like.

"Madrid is very chaotic and expensive," said Su-ok. "We're very lucky to live here. My mother didn't feel safe walking around Madrid after dark. But here a woman can go anywhere without any concerns."

"Did you learn Spanish?" asked Jun-su.

"*Sí*," said Su-ok.

"Ah—fluent!" said Jun-su.

Su-ok bopped him affectionately on the shoulder with the box of sweets and laughed. "What I was trying to say is that one of my classmates was at school with you in Wonsan," she said. "He came to the talk you gave."

"Really?" said Jun-su. For a moment, he couldn't think who it might be. Then a horrible realization dawned on him.

"His name is Seo Tae-il. His father is the Regional Party Chairman."

"Oh yes," said Jun-su, feeling a sour taste at the back of his throat. "Good old Tae-il. Say hi from me."

"I will," said Su-ok. "He's a very gifted hacker."

The headlights of the trolleybus pierced the darkness with their long golden beams. It pulled to a stop in front of them.

"Jun-su, I'm going to the Kaeson funfair next week," said Su-ok. "It's my friend's birthday. Would you like to come? You could bring Mun Jong."

"Definitely," said Jun-su without hesitation. "Consider it confirmed."

Against the black of the lightless city, the bus looked like a tank of fish, lit from within, as it receded into the night.

The Kaeson funfair was in the heart of the city, not far from the enormous Kim Il-sung Stadium where the Mass Games were held each year.

A dozen people went on the trip. Jun-su was pleased he'd brought Jong. Song-chol was amusing, but sometimes childish. Tae-hoon was likable, but a bit plodding. But Mun Jong was funny, and he also had a certain gravity to him. He was the friend you needed in a crisis. Jun-su had even felt able to confide in him about his health problems, and Jong had listened in his usual phlegmatic and reassuring way.

On the excursion, Jun-su saw another side of Su-ok. She was clearly the leader of her friends and it crossed his mind that she was used to getting her own way.

"I gave your regards to Tae-il," she said, taking Jun-su aside as the friends tested their strength against an arm-wrestling machine in the arcade. "It's funny you don't see more of each other, as old school-friends," she mused.

"We weren't close," said Jun-su. "He was sporty and I was more of a nerdy type."

"Jun-su the nerd!" teased Su-ok, but there was affection in her voice.

The funfair was full of exotic amusements: arcade games,

a roller coaster, a rifle range, a toy railway. There were even a few foreign tourists, wandering around in amazement, like astronauts exploring an unfamiliar world. They seemed heavy, pale, and clumsy, as though unaccustomed to the new laws of gravity on this planet.

Jong was the best shot on the rifle range and posed with one of the foreigners for a photo.

The funfair stayed open until eleven. By now it was dark. Su-ok and Jun-su had found themselves separated from the rest of the group. They left the funfair and crossed the road to the park on the other side.

Away from the lights of the rides and amusements, the city was pitch-black. Su-ok's arm brushed Jun-su's as they walked, twice. He gave her more space as they came to a stop under a gingko tree, through whose branches the stars were visible.

"What's wrong with you, Jun-su?" she said quietly.

"Wrong with me?" echoed Jun-su in surprise, turning to look at her.

"Don't you like me?" said Su-ok. She frowned and her face dimly reflected the distant glow of the funfair.

Jun-su kissed her warm mouth and felt her tongue enter his, like a tiny fish. She pulled apart from him and searched his face earnestly with her eyes.

"I love you, Jun-su," she whispered.

"I love you too, plum blossom," he said.

"Plum blossom," she said, stroking his hair. "Such a poet."

* * *

Jun-su felt like he was floating on a pink cloud as he rattled back to campus with Jong on the trolleybus. It was obvious to Jong that something had happened between Jun-su and Su-ok.

"Tell me, brother," said Jong.

"You've got to keep it secret."

"Even the CIA won't get it out of me with torture."

"I kissed Su-ok."

Jong looked a bit sad. "Be careful, brother."

"Why do you say that?"

"She's not like us, brother. You know that."

"She's just the same as anyone else," protested Jun-su.

Jong gave him a wry smile. "You think so?" He gestured discreetly at their fellow passengers. "Are they the same as Su-ok?"

Jun-su looked at the other people in the trolleybus, all sitting in silence. A flash of sparks from the overhead cables crackled outside the window. As the trolleybus turned a corner, the passengers' heads swayed from side to side in unison. The simultaneity of their movements made it seem as though they were somehow part of a single mechanism. Of course they were nothing like Su-ok. No one was. No one he'd ever met had Su-ok's grace, autonomy, and air of privilege.

Jong held his finger to his lips to indicate the conversation was at an end. Then he began humming to himself, a famous tune by the Pochonbo Electronic Ensemble called "The Shoes My Brother Bought Me Fit Tight."

There was no tradition of dating in North Korea, and romance on campus, while not unheard of, was very difficult. The students' free time was limited. Coursework was demanding. There was compulsory political activity, self-criticism every Saturday, and few easy or approved ways for lovers to be alone with one another.

If anything, the impossibility of any consummation gave the love between Jun-su and Su-ok an intense, fairy-tale quality. They volunteered together to work on the brigades of students that spruced up the political monuments in the city. When they had free time, they took long walks along the Pothong River, the slow-moving tributary of the Taedong. They went to the cinema, where they could hold hands in the darkness and, if they were very discreet, kiss.

They were both enthusiastic moviegoers. Together they watched the romantic comedy *On the Green Carpet*, and the classic action movie *Order No. 27*. Both were profoundly moved by a very recent release, *People of Chagang Province*. It was an unusually frank and downbeat film. It showed how farmers in a northern part of the country had suffered during the Arduous March. In one shocking scene, characters ate charcoal to survive. Su-ok came out of the auditorium angry and shaken. "I can never forgive the Yankees for this," she said. "They want to bring our country to its knees."

In the aftermath of the film, Jun-su shared his recollections of the famine in Wonsan with Su-ok. He talked about the awful noise he'd heard from his bedroom window: the wailing of hungry children that had sounded like a chorus of frogs.

Tears sprang to Su-ok's eyes. "That's why our work is so important," she said with great vehemence. She explained that the hackers were working on ways not only to disrupt their enemies' military capability, but also to take the computers that controlled their industry hostage. It would be poetic justice if the hackers could make the Yankee dogs pay money to support the Korean children they had orphaned and starved.

On days they went to the movies, Jun-su would wait for Su-ok outside the computer science faculty as his classes tended to finish earlier.

One day he was standing on the concrete steps when he saw Su-ok emerging from the building with some of her classmates. Beside Su-ok was a tall, strapping student whose deep voice was so loud that Jun-su could hear it from outside.

Jun-su was filled with envy. A possessive urge took hold of him and he suddenly resented her easy familiarity with this student. Su-ok had never given him any reason to doubt her feelings for him, yet he still burned with jealousy.

She and the other student came to a stop beside Jun-su. "I believe you two comrades know each other," she said.

"Hello, brother," said the student. Jun-su now recognized him as Seo Tae-il. He had grown broad-shouldered and square-jawed like a heroic worker in a propaganda poster.

"Hello," said Jun-su, trying to convey a warmth he didn't feel at all. He couldn't help thinking about Seo Tae-il's big hands and how close he was standing to Su-ok.

"We were talking about your presentation in class," Su-ok told Jun-su. "We were praising your English skills. Your old school must be proud of you both: an elite linguist and an elite programmer. There must be something in the water in Wonsan."

Tae-il bowed in mock humility at this compliment.

It was both surprising and annoying. Jun-su had always thought of Tae-il as a plodder. He'd assumed that Tae-il's father's position in the Workers' Party had enabled him to get his son exempted from military service and to wangle him a place at the university. It was galling that Tae-il had turned out not only to have a gift for computing but also to have somehow earned Su-ok's admiration.

"Comrade Tae-il was always an exceptional student," said Jun-su. "He inspired us all by his efforts."

Tae-il smiled, but Jun-su knew from the wary look in his eyes that nothing had been forgotten.

* * *

In mid-June, the students began preparations for their end-of-year exams. One Saturday afternoon, Jun-su collected Su-ok from the library and they went for a walk along the Pothong River. The riverside path was full of fishermen. Jun-su reminisced about his Sunday afternoon fishing trips with his father. "I hope you meet my parents one day," he said.

Jun-su and Su-ok knew that for both of them, whatever happened, marriage was a long way off. The propagandists of the Workers' Party made it clear that it was important to do your duty for the country before entertaining thoughts of settling down. The Great Leader himself had determined that thirty was the appropriate age for a man to take a wife. Jun-su was only just nineteen.

Still, Su-ok responded to the implied promise in Jun-su's words. She took his hand and led him to a viaduct that crossed the river. Its concrete supports screened the young lovers from the passersby. She pulled Jun-su towards her and kissed him.

"Remember when you called me 'plum blossom'?" she said.

"Of course," said Jun-su. "All poets understand the meaning of plum blossom."

In the poetry of East Asia, the pale blossom of the flowering winter plum evokes evanescence and memory, but also rebirth and the promise of new life. For Jun-su it carried bleaker associations too. He wanted to explain everything it represented to Su-ok. Teacher Kang keeling over in his black sack. The House of Possibility. The turbid waters of the East Sea in spring. His pride at his mastery of English. His mother stroking his feverish head. The rattle of the yut sticks on the floor of his parents' apartment. The love he felt for Su-ok.

Leaning against the concrete upright, Su-ok hoisted up her skirt and slipped Jun-su's hand into her underwear. She gasped and closed her eyes as his finger went inside her.

At five o'clock each Sunday afternoon, rain or shine, the Beryllium Boys gathered to sit cross-legged on the floor of their dormitory and play the House of Possibility.

The four friends were in a hurry to finish the campaign before the university broke up for summer and the students were sent to the countryside to help with the harvest. The story had reached a climactic moment. The three adventurers had split up in order to explore an underground complex. Jong, as Gumiho the Bold, was alone in the dungeon.

Jun-su described what he could see.

"Holding his torch aloft, Gumiho turns the blind corner," Jun-su said, lowering his voice to a dramatic whisper as he evoked the scene.

"At its far end, the gallery opens into a vast chamber, stretching away into the shadows. The torchlight plays on glimmers of gold: unworked seams high up in the walls of the cavern; heaps of coins spilling out from sacks onto the floor. There are chests of gold artifacts too. As Gumiho kneels to inspect a scabbard of intricate Elvish work, an axe suddenly swishes across his field of vision, missing his head—just—but knocking the torch from his hand. Gumiho looks up to see the grim face of the troll-king, uglier and more bloodthirsty than the Yankee bastards in the movies. His torch rolls across the floor of the cavern, still lit, shedding its flickering yellow light on two slumped, bloodstained figures. Even in this darkness, Gumiho knows who they are: Kapsberger the Cleric and Elvis the Bard. Alive, but the troll-king's captives! The troll-king holds the blade of the axe to Gumiho's neck. His breath stinks of rotten flesh. 'Serve me, and you will live,' he says."

Jun-su paused to let the gravity of the moment sink in and then followed up with the clincher. "What do you do?" he asked.

"Say yes, then plunge the dagger in his heart," said Song-chol, who played as Elvis the Bard.

"Shut up, fool. You're bound and gagged," Jun-su told him. "Gumiho must make this decision alone."

Jong shook his head and sighed thoughtfully. "It's not an easy matter to attack the troll-king. How many men can I see?"

Jun-su cast the yut sticks behind his hand. His face was expressionless. "None."

Suddenly there was a knock at the door that brought the friends back to reality. Sometimes, after drinking soju all Sunday afternoon, the volleyball players down the hall got confused about which door was which, but this didn't sound like their shambolic drunken knock. It was a crisp rap.

Tae-hoon made his way to the door and opened it. Six members of the Kim Il-sung Socialist Youth League and two men in dark jackets stood at the threshold. "Comrade Cho Jun-su," said one of the men.

Jun-su stood up.

"Come with us," said the visitor.

Jun-su was taken to a featureless concrete building next to the Kimilsungism Study Hall. It was the office of the campus police.

The two *bowibu* men conducted the interrogation. They were tall and solidly built, and moved with the graceful assertiveness of expert taekwondo players. One spoke with a North Hamgyong accent; the other wore a modish short-sleeved jacket that exposed the toned muscles of his forearms. They refused to tell Jun-su their names, so he christened them mentally Mr. North and Inspector Forearms. They said they were putting together a report for the Thought Examination Committee.

Inspector Forearms did most of the talking. To begin with, it was almost leisurely. He seemed fascinated by Jun-su's unusual choice of pastime.

Jun-su gave a detailed but somewhat selective account of

the origin of his interest in the game. Meanwhile, Mr. North flicked through the exercise books that they had taken from the dormitory.

"You call yourself the leader of this game?" said Inspector Forearms, using the Korean word *jidoja* that is applied to the Dear and Great Leaders.

"I'm the *leader*," Jun-su explained, using the English term and trying to avoid any hint of direct contradiction.

"*Leader*," sneered the interrogator. "From what you tell me, it's clear that this game is a Yankee imperialist abomination designed to weaken the people's morality. It teaches violence and acquisitiveness. It undermines belief in our socialist system. Our Dear Leader, Comrade Kim Jong-il, has instructed us to protect the pure hearts of the Korean people from reactionary propaganda. Your own evidence condemns you. Elvis the Bard—do you deny this is an American name?"

Jun-su suppressed a sigh. He hated the name Elvis the Bard, but it was something that Song-chol had insisted on: a pointless flight of whimsy that was typical of him. "There's been a misunderstanding, comrade," he said. "I recently gave a talk to Professor Hwang's students at the computer science faculty. I'm trying to help the work of the Fatherland."

"Don't drag Professor Hwang into this, you scum," said Mr. North, looking up from a notebook. "Where did you get all this information from?"

"I have a copy of the English text. I translated it."

Mr. North snorted. "That's the first word of truth you've spoken." He reached down to a vinyl sports bag at his feet and pulled something out. "Do you recognize this?"

Jun-su felt his heart flutter and he was overcome with dizziness.

Mr. North unwrapped the paper cover. It was already half off, and he removed it roughly so the aged and brittle paper tore. Underneath was Jun-su's precious book and the cover showing the red troll. In the context of the interrogation, the image suddenly seemed like an obvious and poisonous attack on the country's socialist ideals.

"Can I have a drink of water?" asked Jun-su.

"You can have water after you've answered the question."

"Yes," said Jun-su quietly. "That's my book. Professor Hwang—"

Mr. North slapped Jun-su's face so hard that he saw stars. "Say his name again—I dare you!" he said. "That man is a Hero of Socialist Labor. You are a reactionary traitor."

"No," protested Jun-su.

"Do you deny that you learned this game from the traitor and pervert Kang Yeong-nam—a man who was later unmasked as a Yankee spy?"

"It was Teacher Kang who first taught me the game," said Jun-su. "I was eleven or twelve and I was ill. He was treating me with needles."

"Why would you need an old pervert to treat you with needles when the socialist Fatherland provides everyone with free healthcare?" said Mr. North.

Every conceivable answer to that question left Jun-su in greater jeopardy. "I don't know," he said feebly.

"Who else have you introduced to this game?" asked Inspector Forearms.

"Just the men you saw playing."

"Really?" said Mr. North. "No others?"

"No," said Jun-su. He was determined to keep Su-ok's name out of this.

Mr. North took a block of paper out of his holdall and placed it in front of Jun-su along with an assortment of pens.

The paper was of the highest quality, smooth and white. Jun-su ran his finger across it and thought of Su-ok's skin.

"We're going to need a letter of self-reflection from you," said Inspector Forearms. "Conduct self-criticism."

"But I haven't done anything wrong," said Jun-su.

"Citizen," said Mr. North, "nothing proclaims your guilt more loudly than your fake attempts to seem ignorant of your crime. We know what you've done. You know what you've done. You need to confess it. If you want a model for your letter, I suggest you take a look at this."

The inspector pulled some handwritten papers from the bag at his feet. He placed them in front of Jun-su. With a terrible pang of recognition, Jun-su saw that the handwriting was his mother's.

* * *

Jun-su was moved that evening to a detention center north of Pyongyang in the back of a windowless van that stank of vomit. The work of the Thought Examination Committee continued.

It was clear to Jun-su by now that Seo Tae-il had triggered the investigation against him. He fully understood why, though he lacked the precise vocabulary to explain it. A shameful thing had occurred between Seo Tae-il and Teacher Kang. Jun-su had guessed enough of it to be a threat. Now Tae-il was following the logic of survival in their world: destroying someone who had the potential to destroy him.

Aside from Tae-il, no one wanted to see Jun-su punished for playing his game, but everyone knew how these things worked. Jun-su was being swept away by an inexorable force. He was drowning in a torrential river and anyone who reached out a hand to help him ran the risk of drowning too.

Mr. North and Inspector Forearms continued to interrogate him at his new location, sometimes working together, sometimes alternating. Jun-su never slept for more than two hours and he quickly lost track of time.

The inspectors would periodically read other people's testimony to him. It shocked Jun-su to learn that the *bowibu* had been building their case against him for months. The statements they'd collected were anonymized, but it was clear from the details who the speakers were. All the Beryllium Boys had made statements that the interrogators used against him.

"Witness D said, and I quote, 'He told me he learned the game from a dirty old man in Wonsan,' unquote. Do you deny this, citizen?"

With a wrench, Jun-su recognized it as a sentence he'd said to Su-ok. He recalled saying it as part of an intimate conversation they'd had about their respective childhoods. Su-ok had shared a confidence about a precocious romance she'd had with a classmate called Raimundo at the International School in Madrid. It was a story that seemed steeped in Spanish glamour. Unable to top it, Jun-su had countered with a self-deprecating anecdote about his provincial upbringing, in which he'd joked that its high point was learning the House of Possibility from a dirty old man. Stripped of all nuance, the remark seemed harsh, decadent, and incriminating.

Any attempt to disagree with the interrogators was met with an immediate physical response. They beat him if he contradicted them directly; they beat him harder if he seemed to contradict them by stealth.

On the former occasions, they beat him languidly, aiming heavy, emotionless blows at his kidneys. The lack of venom in the punches paradoxically made them more efficient: the relaxed, whipping motion of Mr. North's arms penetrated deep inside his body.

But when they thought he was being a clever dick, was trying to get around the allegations by sophistry, they beat him with real animosity. Mr. North would mockingly repeat his pleas for understanding—"That's not exactly right"; "It's more complicated than that"; "Things didn't happen in that order"—and even Jun-su heard the whining defensiveness of his rationalizations. Nothing angered them more than his pleas for nuance and context.

The Great Leader had said that all citizens had two lives: their biological life, which was given to them by their parents, and their political life, which was more important and ultimately determined their worth as a human being.

As Jun-su lay on the floor after one of these beatings, he understood that his torturers were acting out of the deepest sincerity. They wanted to help him and they were prepared to risk his biological existence in order to give him a chance to redeem his political one.

His crimes were clear: he had protected a spy and known traitor with his silence; he had made translations and disseminated a banned text; he had attempted to undermine the morale of the Korean people with counterrevolutionary propaganda.

Mr. North was full of genuine contempt for Jun-su: he'd jeopardized the well-being of people he claimed to love.

But there was also a tone of prurience and repressed desire in some of his accusations. "Did you try to have sex with Ri Su-ok, you dirty pervert?"

"I never touched her," said Jun-su. He was haunted by the thought of Su-ok undergoing her own form of this interrogation: her delicate body being punched and kicked by Mr. North's pointed dress shoes.

He understood there was only one form of expiation he could offer. When the beatings had subsided, and his interrogators recognized his desire to make a sincere repentance, he gripped the cheap ballpoint pen in his bruised hand and wrote his confession with the same care that he'd devoted to his translation of the *Dungeon Masters Guide* in the Wonsan Library.

Mr. North stood over him as he wrote and removed each finished page as soon as it was completed.

"This is good," he said. "This is good, citizen. There is hope for you yet."

# THE SHOES MY BROTHER BOUGHT ME FIT TIGHT

Jun-su was never entirely sure where his interrogation took place. There are at least two *bowibu*-run detention centers near Pyongyang that fit the description. From accounts I've read elsewhere, I think it's most likely that he was held in one in the suburb of Yonsong. This location—wherever it was geographically—marked the end of a period of Jun-su's life that he would look back to, in the years to come, with mingled shame and nostalgia.

It was late summer 2003 when Jun-su was driven out of the capital on the bed of a six-wheel ZIL truck. With him under the roof of faded green canvas were almost two dozen other prisoners, including a family of Christians, the extended family of some attempted refugees who had been repatriated from China, and the former manager of a Pyongyang power plant who had fallen into disgrace. He was accompanied by his wife and daughter. Jun-su later learned that this man had been sentenced for stealing the property of the Korean people. In fact, his actual crime had been to use a homemade electric blanket to warm up his bed—a violation of government policy on conserving energy.

Outside the capital, the harvest was under way and the fields were full of people. It gave the guards an excuse to abuse the prisoners for being idle while the rest of the country was laboring to feed the nation—as though being sent to prison were a ruse to avoid work! Jun-su knew that some of his university comrades were among the workers in the fields. He wondered if they were aware of what was happening to him. He thought of the way he'd compartmentalized his own internal life, how he'd arranged things so his undeniable knowledge of arrests, disappearances, and executions was never openly examined; so he'd never had to face difficult questions about the regime—and his own complicity with it.

Their destination was in the far north of the country, close to the Chinese border. It was a vast penal colony, the size of a district, surrounded by barbed wire and subdivided into a number of smaller villages. Some of the villages were for individual prisoners; others had been built to house entire families who were tainted by the guilt of a single member.

On arrival at the camp, guards divided the prisoners into two groups. The larger group, which included all the Christians, was sent to the Zone of Total Control, from which there was virtually no possibility of release. Jun-su and five others were taken to a village in the Rerevolutionizing Zone, where, through political reeducation and hard work, they had a slim chance of winning their freedom.

Any sense of hopefulness this raised was quickly dashed by the conditions in their new home. Jun-su found himself in a barracks set on one side of a long, narrow valley. It held about a thousand prisoners, all men. He was horrified by the emaciated state of his fellow inmates. Most were undersized, all were skeletally thin, and many were missing fingers or hands.

At five o'clock the morning after his arrival, Jun-su and the four other men in the unit he'd been assigned to marched from the barracks to a nearby gypsum quarry where they began chipping away at the white rock with hand tools. The blocks of gypsum were broken down into smaller pieces, which were then ground by hand into dust and scooped into sacks to be used as fertilizer. The work unit leader, Han Young-sun, allocated the tools to the men at roll call and took them back at the end of the day. He was also responsible for the team meeting its production quota. The men worked until 7 p.m. and then marched back to the barracks for dinner. After food, there were two hours of self-criticism and political reeducation. This consisted of prisoners complaining that other prisoners weren't working hard enough and readings from the newspaper.

The food rations were so small that the prisoners were constantly on the brink of starvation. They went to extraordinary lengths to supplement their diet: eating insects and tree bark, trapping rats to broil on shovels over open fires, and collecting the undigested kernels of corn from animal droppings. Even then, Jun-su lost so much weight that he had to cinch the waist of his gray trousers with twine. Given his physical infirmity, he was certain that his death was not far away.

Lying exhausted on his cot in the stink of the barracks at the end of each day, Jun-su understood that his life had come to an end. He was no longer a person. He was a thing without agency. He found it too painful to dwell on thoughts of Ri Su-ok. Instead he conjured memories of his childhood. He recalled a golden age before the death of the Great Leader when there was pollock soup, candy once a month, and white rice on Saturday, and he had basked in the adoration of his parents.

Winter came. A blizzard blocked the entrance to the valley and Jun-su's work unit was assigned to clear the snow from the access road. The team was watched constantly by two guards who wouldn't hesitate to beat the prisoners if they felt they were slacking.

As the men worked, the snowstorm increased in intensity. Looking back down the valley towards the village, Jun-su saw that their tracks had been erased. It felt as if he was witnessing his own annihilation. The distant huts vanished as the blizzard closed in on them. Jun-su could just hear the breathing of the prisoner working to his left, and occasionally glimpsed his rag-covered hands brushing aside the snow.

The end had finally arrived. In a moment, Jun-su would fall into the snow and die. His clothes would be stripped from his corpse and his body would be thrown into the pit behind the latrines. As he felt himself surrendering to this anonymous and shameful destiny, a pair of shadowy wings seemed to enfold him and from somewhere in the distance he heard the clattering of yut sticks.

The sixteenth of February 2012 was a bright and bitterly cold midwinter day. After a breakfast of corn porridge and cabbage soup, the prisoners in Jun-su's section were gathered together and marched over the pass into the next valley, where another, larger village stood around a timber mill.

Walking up the slope, Jun-su looked across to the spot where, a lifetime earlier, he had been sent to clear snow with his work unit.

Of the five men on that detail, three had subsequently died. One had been executed for collecting fallen chestnuts without authorization. Another had choked to death after having his mouth smashed in with a stick as a punishment. His crime: stealing a leather whip, boiling it until it was soft, and then eating it. Jun-su couldn't remember what had happened to the third man.

The prisoners reached the crest of the hill, descended to the village on the other side, and assembled in a square of packed snow where they were made to sit. The mill was silent; work had stopped, but the smell of cut timber perfumed the valley.

Jun-su's assumption was they were going to be made to watch another execution. In a moment, a terrified prisoner would be dragged before the crowd, denounced for stealing food or trying to escape, and then hanged. Sometimes the other prisoners would be encouraged to strike the corpse as they were filed past afterwards for a closer look.

On this occasion, however, a well-fed man in a fur-collared coat and a flat cap stood before them. Puffs of frosty breath punctuated his words. He reminded the assembled prisoners of the significance of the date. It was the Day of the Shining Star, the birthday of the Dear Leader, Kim Jong-il, whose death the previous year had come as a tremendous blow to his people. Exactly seventy years earlier, he continued, the Dear Leader had been born on the slopes of Mount Paektu as his parents led the fight to liberate Korea from the Japanese imperialist dogs.

The Dear Leader, the speaker explained—though everyone knew the story—had devoted his life to continuing the work of his father, to safeguarding the achievements of the Kim Il-sung nation. It was a noble and difficult struggle that had now passed into the hands of the Supreme Leader, Comrade Marshal Kim Jong-un. In recognition of the Dear Leader's birthday and as a reward for the hard work of self-criticism and the great strides he had made in rerevolutionizing his consciousness, the speaker was glad to announce, one of the prisoners was today going to leave the camp and rejoin the Kim Il-sung nation.

He paused for effect and looked out at the faces in front of him. Then he called Cho Jun-su to join him.

The announcement brought no apparent joy to Jun-su's fellow prisoners. Each of them must have privately hoped that his name would be on the speaker's lips.

Cho Jun-su was made to swear an oath of loyalty to the Democratic People's Republic. He was given a travel pass, a ration card, and a bundle of clothes by a female guard he didn't recognize.

"How do you feel, Comrade Jun-su?" the man in the coat asked expansively.

Cho Jun-su was utterly baffled and unable to comprehend the news, but he realized that this was not the response the occasion required. "I feel joy and immense gratitude to our Supreme Leader, Comrade Marshal Kim Jong-un, and I promise to do my best," he shouted.

The prisoners were dismissed and the inmates from Jun-su's village stood up and marched away without him.

Jun-su was left alone with the guards and the man in the coat. He followed them into the administrative building where he was instructed to bathe and change into his new clothes.

When he came out of the bathroom, his old clothes were gone and so was his travel pass. This made him nervous. It felt entirely possible that the whole event had been a charade and he was about to be executed anyway.

The prison guard brought a bowl of soup. When he had finished it, she refilled the bowl.

"I don't have a travel pass," said Jun-su. "Someone's taken it."

"You don't need it," said the woman. "They're sending a car for you."

The car was a shiny Pyeonghwa Pronto, a big SUV that looked shockingly out of place in the squalor of the camp. Its driver, Mr. Shin, was brushing snow off the hood when Jun-su came out of the administrator's hut. Mr. Shin's plump cheeks, his thick jacket and fur-lined gloves, and his gleaming vehicle made him seem like a different species from the filthy, emaciated prisoners. He wrinkled up his nose when Jun-su got into the car. Jun-su realized that the stink of the camp still clung to him. Even his new set of clothes seemed shabby and incongruous against the smart upholstery.

"I brought you some of my wife's soup," Mr. Shin said. "You look like you could do with it."

"Funnily enough," said Jun-su, "I've just had some."

Mr. Shin shrugged and put the thermos back in the footwell. He didn't say much until they'd passed through the final checkpoint and were driving over the unpaved road beyond the camp.

"My brother-in-law was sent away to the mountains," Mr. Shin said. "How long were you there?"

"Nine years," said Jun-su, but as he said the words, he felt almost certain that he had known no other life than the camp. All his earlier memories belonged to someone else, a naïve boy whose frivolity and lack of insight now broke his heart.

After two hours of driving, they left the unpaved roads and joined an empty highway. They drove for another four hours, occasionally passing the outskirts of small towns, or pausing at checkpoints, where Mr. Shin showed the guards his documents. Finally, towards evening, Mr. Shin pulled up at an attractive modernist building of curved concrete and smart picture windows. "This is your destination," said Mr. Shin.

Built in the 1960s with the help of Russian money and advisers, it was the Red Harvest Sanatorium, a medical center for the country's elite. Outside, a large mural showed the Great Leader giving a team of its white-coated medical personnel some on-the-spot guidance.

Inside, a doctor and a dentist examined Jun-su. Naturally, he was severely underweight and malnourished. His body bore the scars of multiple beatings. He had lost two toes on his left foot to frostbite. But, according to the doctor, there was no longer any sign of the heart murmur that had tormented him since childhood.

The sanatorium's personnel expressed no surprise at his condition. They took impressions of his mouth in order to make him a set of false teeth, gave him pills for intestinal parasites, and dosed him with cod-liver oil.

Jun-su was shown to a whitewashed room. Unusually, it had a bed as well as a small desk, and an adjoining bathroom. A door opened onto a balcony that looked out towards a range of mountains covered with larches. There were no portraits on the wall, only a map of the sanatorium grounds that had recommended walks marked in red. A wardrobe contained clothes Jun-su's size: underwear, shirts, trousers, even a thick overcoat and outdoor shoes.

Squatting in his bathtub, Jun-su worked at his skin with a nailbrush until he'd removed the ingrained dirt of a decade. The enamel squeaked as he stood up and stepped out of the bath. Within twelve hours, he'd used more hot water than he had in the previous ten years. Wiping the steam off the bathroom mirror, Jun-su gazed into an unfamiliar face. It seemed miraculous that, after all that time, he was still a young man. For the first moment since he'd left the prison, he allowed himself a feeling of hope.

Physically Jun-su might have been free, but his internal world still belonged to the camp.

The sanatorium had a restaurant where its half dozen guests ate at separate tables. Each was served a specific meal designed by the sanatorium's nutritionists.

One of the other guests was an obese middle-aged man with a florid complexion that suggested high blood pressure. At mealtimes he was served very small portions. He finished his food quickly, then sat in his seat fuming and glancing around the room. His greed and entitlement reminded Jun-su of the officials at whose drunken gatherings in Wonsan he had recited his patriotic verses. Seeing the huge piles of sweet potatoes, nut paste, and fish that had been prescribed to Jun-su, the man grew indignant and called over one of the staff.

Jun-su couldn't hear the whole conversation, but the sound of the man's North Hamgyong accent triggered a repressed memory from his first interrogation. Suddenly Jun-su recalled being restrained by two guards, stripped naked, and Mr. North burning the pubic hair off his testicles with a cigarette lighter.

During the days, Jun-su was allowed to roam around the grounds of the sanatorium. He would walk in the cold air for hours, hoping to exhaust himself so that he would sleep deeply. But he was so accustomed to the noise and activity of the barracks, the breathing of his fellow inmates, that the silence of his room unsettled him.

The unreality of his surroundings and the abruptness of the change were too much for him to process. The doctor gave him sleeping pills, but they had no effect. Jun-su started to unravel. He'd think about his parents and grow panicky. He became obsessed with the thought that he was already dead. At night he lay awake staring at a mysterious blue light on the ceiling. It was part of the sanatorium's alarm system.

Finally, when he was having his blood pressure taken one morning, he broke down in tears and pleaded with one of the female orderlies: "What's happening to me?"

The orderly smiled uncomfortably and fetched a senior doctor.

"Comrade Jun-su, how can I help?" asked the doctor.

"I can't sleep. The pills aren't working," said Jun-su.

"No problem. We'll try you on some zolpidem tartrate. I use it myself occasionally. It should guarantee you five hours' deep sleep."

"The other thing is . . ." Jun-su looked at the doctor. "I'm not sure what I'm doing here."

"We understand you were involved in some kind of accident," said the doctor, as though reading from a script that he didn't quite believe. "You were carrying out some duties for the Fatherland, during which you were injured. We've been instructed to give you the best medical care we have so you can continue with your important work."

Jun-su took one of the pills after his evening meal. It didn't have any effect, so he took another. The next thing he knew, he seemed to be lying on his mattress in his parents' flat in Wonsan, ready to get up and go to school. He heard a polite cough.

It was the orderly, Miss Roh. She told him he'd been asleep for twelve hours.

Thanks to his new teeth and drastically improved diet, Jun-su quickly gained weight. The hairdresser neatened his prison crew cut as it grew out into a short back and sides. The pills regulated his sleep and Jun-su's physical health began to return.

During the days, Jun-su read novels from the sanatorium library and went for long walks along the marked trails. The most ambitious one led up the nearest mountain. Steps had been cut to help the walkers ascend the steepest sections, and the sides of the path were banked with logs to prevent erosion. It had all been constructed by hand. It was the kind of hard labor that, until a few weeks earlier, Jun-su had been doing with the other men in his work unit.

The thaw was under way. The moist air seemed more raw and cold than it had during the days of hard frost. The damp had also released the scent of the larches and the leaf-mold underfoot.

Jun-su felt his heart beating as he walked uphill. For so many years in the camp, he'd expected it to give out at any minute. It was one of the things that had helped make his incarceration bearable. *When my body's had enough,* he had told himself, *it will set me free.*

At the end of the path stood a little clearing with a wooden bench that looked out over the mountains. As he neared it to take a seat, Jun-su noticed something move on the edge of the forest. Jun-su froze. A fox, its orange ears tipped with black flashes, milky-white fur on its chest, turned its triangular muzzle towards him. For a moment, it held his gaze with its steady hazel eyes; then it turned and stalked away into the forest.

Though he was not conventionally superstitious, Jun-su ascribed great significance to the appearance of that fox.

In Korean folklore the Gumiho, or nine-tailed fox, is a mythical creature that symbolizes transformation, deception, and longevity. Its appearance is considered somewhat ominous. But Jun-su felt differently about this animal: it seemed like an emblem of hope. In almost every culture, the fox holds a special fascination for human beings. The fox is rarely the most powerful animal in its ecosystem, so it relies for survival on cunning and adaptability—hence its sense of kinship with humans, who occupy a similar position in the hierarchy of predators.

Standing in the dripping woods, Jun-su followed the animal with his eyes. As powerless as he still was, he understood that he was a survivor, and he swore that he would adapt like a fox to whatever possibilities lay ahead of him.

When he got back to the sanatorium, he passed Miss Roh in the lobby. "Something arrived for you," she said.

A sealed cardboard box stood in the corner of Jun-su's bedroom. It was addressed to him by name in thick black characters. Jun-su went back to the lobby and asked Miss Roh for a pair of scissors. As she gave them to him, she shot him a look that was full of sly curiosity.

Jun-su locked his door, knelt beside the box, and sawed through the thick tape that almost covered the cardboard. Finally he folded open the flaps and peered inside. It was packed with polystyrene chips. On top of them lay a printed note in English.

*Please familiarize yourself with these,* it said.

Jun-su delved into the polystyrene chips. Inside was a second, much smaller package. This was dense and heavy. From its address label, written in English, it appeared to have been sent from Luxembourg to an apartment complex in Geneva. Jun-su could barely venture a guess how it had got from there to the sanatorium.

It contained a slipcase holding three hardback books.

Their pages had a satiny finish that invited his touch. Flipping through them brought on an overwhelming sense of nostalgia. They were the rule books for the House of Possibility—not quite the game that he and Teacher Kang had conspired over, but the version as it was played in 2012.

Reading the books, Jun-su quickly became aware that his English had atrophied during the years in the camp. His brain was like a stiff muscle that had lost its range of movement. The sanatorium's library had no English dictionary, so Jun-su requested one from his doctor. He also asked for a pen and paper so he could take notes.

When the maid came to clean his room the next morning, Jun-su noticed her eyeing the box. "That would be good to store winter clothes in," she said.

Jun-su took the hint. "It's just getting in the way," he said. "If you can find any use for it, you're welcome to have it."

The maid knelt beside the box and began scooping the polystyrene chips into one of the plastic bags that she used to line the bins. As she reached inside the box, her hands brushed against something and she cried out: "Sir! You've forgotten these." She placed two small items on Jun-su's desk, then folded the box flat, bowed, and left the room with it under her arm.

Jun-su examined the objects. One was a small plastic case that held seven dice of different shapes. They were a clear, emerald green and as hard as glass.

The other item made Jun-su catch his breath. It was a small tin tea-caddy of *maehwacha*.

He boiled a kettle and steeped a spoonful of the tea in a glass of hot water. The smell of honey rose from the infusion.

As he stirred the tea with a spoon, white petals began to rehydrate and spin inside the glass. They were the dried flowers of winter plum. *Plum blossom.*

It was April when Mr. Shin came back to collect him. "You look like a new man," said Mr. Shin. He'd brought a suitcase with him for Jun-su's clothes, which he put into the back of the car, a Mercedes.

"What happened to the other one?" Jun-su asked, gesturing at the vehicle.

Mr. Shin shook his head. After checking that no one else was in earshot, he sighed. "I'd give every drop of the blood in my veins for the Fatherland," he said, "but the cars we make are pieces of shit."

Something about Mr. Shin's artless honesty made Jun-su think of his father. He was racked with a sudden pang of longing for his parents. Throughout all those years in the camp, the political meetings had kept him in touch with the changes in leadership, new policies, and adjustments to the party line, but he had received not a word from or about his mother and father. Where were they? What had happened to them? His dearest hope was that they had been spared collective punishment for his crimes.

The car had special license plates that bore the prefix 216—the day of the Dear Leader's birth. These meant it was waved through the checkpoints along the empty highway. After a couple of hours, they drove into a big compound on the outskirts of Pyongyang. High brick walls surrounded an acre of land in which were set a large detached two-story house and a number of smaller outbuildings.

Mr. Shin pulled up outside the main house and popped the latch of the trunk with a switch on the dashboard.

White marble steps led up to the building's entrance. Mr. Shin brushed off Jun-su's attempt to carry his own suitcase. Jun-su followed him inside.

Beyond the vestibule, the lower floor was a sweeping, open-plan living space that looked out onto an impeccable garden. But what really amazed Jun-su were the guitars: dozens of them, hanging on the walls and resting in stands on the floor. A few were acoustic, but most of them were electric ones. Some were wooden with the aged patina of old furniture; others brand-new and glowing with the iridescent colors of tropical fish: orange, sky blue, and blood red. One was even shaped like a bolt of lightning.

"Someone here likes guitars," said Jun-su.

Mr. Shin stopped and turned his head sharply. "You think so?"

As Jun-su looked at him, Mr. Shin raised a forefinger slowly to his lips and held it there. He waited until Jun-su nodded to signify that he'd understood the message: this was not a place where one could speak freely.

At the far end of the room stood a set of black speaker cabinets, piled on top of each other. There were nine cabinets, in three stacks of three boxes. On the front of every one the word *Marshall* was picked out in flowing white roman letters.

Jun-su wanted to ask Mr. Shin which Marshall it referred to, but he thought better of it.

Mr. Shin showed Jun-su to a bedroom on the upper floor,

with windows overlooking the garden. Gazing out over the lawn, Jun-su could see two armed men standing guard by the outer wall.

He struggled to take in the opulence of his new surroundings. His room was enormous. The adjoining tiled bathroom was as big as his bedroom at the sanatorium and had Japanese fittings.

Mr. Shin bowed in farewell. "Good luck," he said.

Jun-su unpacked his things and put them away in the drawers. He hung the new clothes that he still barely recognized as his in the huge walk-in closet.

When he'd finished, he picked up the remote control from the bedside table and switched on the television.

It was unlike any television he'd ever seen—and not just because of its extraordinary size and resemblance to a cinema screen.

The set that came to life on the wall of his bedroom had unfettered access to broadcasters beyond North Korea.

It had the BBC News, CNN, music channels, channels from Germany, Italy, and China—and, most eerie of all for Jun-su, channels from South Korea. As he watched, he wondered if, behind the scenes of prosperity and freedom on the screen, South Korea had labor camps where starving men were beaten to death for stealing food.

At noon, a maid knocked on his door and told him lunch would be served downstairs.

He ate alone, on a big glass table in an empty dining room. The meal was enormous—white rice, braised pork, a dozen vegetable side dishes—but the maid kept apologizing for its simplicity. She spoke halting Korean and the two of them had some difficulty communicating. Jun-su would eventually learn that most of the staff in his new residence were from Thailand and Vietnam.

Late in the afternoon, there was the sound of a car pulling up outside and voices in the hall. Sitting in the museum of guitars, reading a book about rock music in English that he'd found on a coffee table, Jun-su felt suddenly anxious. He stood up, sat down, and stood up again.

A woman in a black skirt suit entered the hallway. She was talking loudly on a mobile phone as she took off her shoes.

When she saw Jun-su, she blushed. "I've got to go," she said, and ended her call.

"Hello, Su-ok," said Jun-su. He marveled at how little she'd changed. During the years of his incarceration, he'd struggled to recall her face. Somehow he could only ever remember it piecemeal: her lips in profile, the smooth skin between her hairline and her temple, her warm, skeptical eyes.

"Hello, Jun-su," she said. "Let me show you the garden."

* * *

The grass of the lawn was so green that Jun-su could imagine, in the hungrier parts of his life, wanting to get down on all fours and eat it like lettuce. A rectangular pond was teeming with fat carp, white and gold.

"The white ones are mine, the gold ones are Jimi's," Su-ok said, taking a handful of fish food from a brushed steel bin beside the water. As she sprinkled the pellets in the pond, pouting mouths broke the surface with audible pops.

Jun-su noticed that the compound's security men were watching from a distance as Su-ok fed the fish. "I'm going to assume that Jimi is your husband," he said.

"That depends on your definition of husband," said Su-ok.

Jun-su took a handful of pellets and threw them into the water. "This place is nice," he said, with more politeness than enthusiasm.

"It was a gift from Jimi's brother."

Jun-su gave her a puzzled look.

"Nanugi," said Su-ok quietly, flicking another handful of pellets over the pond.

Jun-su had to suppress his astonishment. Nanugi—*the one who shares*—was the nickname of the country's Supreme Leader, Comrade Marshal Kim Jong-un. Then, as Jun-su cast his mind back across the chain of events that had taken place since he had left the camp, it struck him that he had been a fool. The source of his patronage should have been obvious. The only people in his country who could possibly live in this much luxury were members of its royal family. The word *Marshall* on the speakers now made perfect sense.

"You can ask me anything," said Su-ok. "We can talk freely here, just not in the house."

"I think I understand," said Jun-su.

"Do you?" said Su-ok quietly. There was a flash of something like anger or bitterness in her voice. "What do you understand, Comrade Jun-su?"

Jun-su was silent for a while. "Maybe you think you've suffered, Su-ok," he said finally. "I don't know if you're a guest or a captive here. But you can't compare this life, whatever it is, with what I lived through. For nine years, I've lived like one of your pet carp, battling for space with other fish, gobbling whatever food came my way." Jun-su stopped himself. There was so much more he wanted to say, but he was afraid to begin revisiting the pain and degradation of those years. "What about my mother and father?" he said. "Is there any news of them?"

"No," said Su-ok, wiping the crumbs delicately from her hands. "I don't know anything. I'm sorry."

Jun-su nodded. "You'd better tell me what's expected of me," he said.

The guests began arriving at 9 p.m. The first to show up was a man in his early thirties called Guk-ju. Urbane, chubby, and pockmarked, he arrived in his own Italian sports car—a sign of extraordinarily high status. He greeted Su-ok with great warmth, threw himself on one of the long couches, and began flicking through a copy of *Paris Match* that he took out of the pocket of his linen jacket.

One of the staff immediately brought over a tumbler of whiskey and ice. Guk-ju accepted it without thanks. "Su-ok tells me you're a poet," he said, not looking up from the pages of his magazine.

"I haven't written any for a while," said Jun-su.

"That's good. I hate poetry," said Guk-ju matter-of-factly.

"I promise not to inflict any on you, in that case," said Jun-su.

The ice tinkled in Guk-ju's tumbler as he sipped. He gazed past Jun-su towards Su-ok, who was supervising the laying of the big glass table. "He's very diplomatic," said Guk-ju. "I like that."

"Don't distract me, Guk-ju. I've lost count of the side dishes," said Su-ok.

"I really don't know what to expect from this," said Guk-ju. "The whole idea of make-believe unnerves me."

"Why is that?" said Jun-su, who was nursing a glass of orange juice.

"Probably because it reminds me of my work," said Guk-ju.

The other two guests were a couple, also in their early thirties, called Sun-kuk and Hyon-ran. Sun-kuk was quiet and reserved. His partner was taller than him and thin, but a prominent bump showed that Hyon-ran was pregnant. She sat beside Sun-kuk and drank fizzy water. Occasionally Sun-kuk rested his hand on her bump with a distracted sense of ownership.

There was still no sign of Jimi. It was almost ten by the time his car appeared. He was in his early thirties too, dressed in a leather jacket, his hair fashionably tousled. Most unusual of all, he wore a gold hoop earring in his left earlobe. To Jun-su, he looked dazzlingly exotic.

"I hope you didn't start without me," he said. He embraced Guk-ju and nodded a vague greeting in the direction of the other guests.

Su-ok had seen to it that one end of the vast table was laid with sushi, pizza, and French wine.

The other end was kept free so the six of them could sit and play the House of Possibility.

Jun-su had decided to run a version of his first-ever adventure: the one he'd played with Teacher Kang back in his parents' apartment in Wonsan. He handed the five character sheets he'd prepared to his novice players and explained the rudiments of the game to them.

They listened intently, and Jun-su found his old enthusiasm for the game reawakening. He could see how much his players enjoyed slipping into another self and entering a world where they were swept along by the undercurrents of their collective imagination.

For almost two hours they were seduced by the freedom of the game's make-believe world. There was something funny about these privileged members of the elite pretending to be impoverished adventurers, running around a desolate village in the countryside—the kind of place they would never visit in real life.

Then suddenly, in the middle of the game, Jimi's interest seemed to flag. He yawned, stood up, and wandered over to his collection of guitars. He took one down from the wall, slung it over his shoulders and plugged a lead into his speakers. The loud buzzing noise that filled the room made everyone cover their ears. Jimi smiled, adjusted the volume, and played a couple of jangly chords.

"What kind of music do you like, Jun-su?" he asked.

Jun-su's mind was blank. He couldn't think of any kind of music. There had been some martial songs played at the camp on special occasions, but on the whole music was one of those aspects of life that had simply ceased to exist for the prisoners.

Jimi damped the strings with his palm and strummed the instrument in bursts of rhythmic clicks. "Say a song you like and I'll play it."

"Anything?" said Jun-su. The other guests were staring at Jun-su, their curiosity about him now undisguised.

"Test me," said Jimi. "I like a challenge."

Jun-su looked at the guitars with their iridescent colors and an old memory stirred. He remembered kissing Su-ok, all those years ago at the Kaeson funfair, and riding home on the trolleybus, half-drunk with joy. He saw Mun Jong's sad face gazing out of the window of the bus as he hummed a tune.

"How about 'The Shoes My Brother Bought Me Fit Tight'?" he said finally.

Guk-ju made a snorting sound, which he disguised as a cough. Jun-su saw a panicked look cross Su-ok's face.

Jimi leaned forward over his guitar. "Is your friend teasing me, Su-ok?" he asked.

"No. Of course not. He's not like that," said Su-ok.

"You want Fatherland music, I'll give you Fatherland music," said Jimi. He scratched his head with his pick and then started playing a melody on the upper frets. It wasn't the song Jun-su had asked for, it was a different tune by the Pochonbo Electronic Ensemble. Jimi's fingers moved loosely and swiftly across the guitar, faster than thought. He bent the strings and closed his eyes as the notes sounded. He shook his head as he added some tremolo. The song altered as he played; now it had become something else that Jun-su couldn't recognize, something that felt dangerously earnest and yearning. He glanced at the other guests for a clue as to how he should behave. They were all listening in silence.

Jimi played for about ten minutes; then Su-ok called the staff in to clear the table and the gathering broke up. Guk-ju, Hyon-ran, and Sun-kuk said their good-byes.

Guk-ju thanked Jun-su for organizing the game. "I loved

it," he said. "It's a combination of fiction and statistics, my two favorite things. And I forgive you the poetry."

After the guests had gone, Su-ok sat beside Jimi on the sofa as he noodled away on one of the acoustic guitars.

"Good night," said Jun-su.

Jimi didn't look up, but he laid the guitar aside and put his hand around Su-ok's wrist.

Even with the door of his bedroom closed, Jun-su could hear the sound of them having sex on the sofa.

The next morning, Jun-su came downstairs to find Su-ok in a skirt and jacket, making espresso from little foil-covered capsules. He could see that her clothes were expensively tailored and made out of fine material that followed the curves of her figure. Her body was less plump and more angular than he remembered, which he thought was a pity.

"Will you drink coffee?" she asked.

"No, thank you," said Jun-su. "I like to drink this in the morning." He showed her the caddy of plum blossom tea.

Su-ok held his gaze, but her face was blank. "Guk-ju sent me a message," she said. "He told me he enjoyed meeting you and he wants to see you for lunch."

"Why?" said Jun-su.

"I expect he sees something in you. It would be a good idea to go. This is the address." Su-ok slid the business card of a restaurant along the countertop. "I'll have the driver take you." The dark-brown coffee left stains on Su-ok's pearly teeth. "It's good news," she said. "It means the evening was a success."

There was no sign of Jimi at all.

Jun-su dressed carefully in one of the suits that hung in his wardrobe. He pinned a badge of the Great Leader over his heart. He thought how strange it was that he'd gone to sleep listening to the sound of the Great Leader's grandson having loud, proprietary sex with the woman Jun-su loved.

The restaurant was not as opulent as Jimi's home, but it was smart and new and full of the capital's business elite. These were the *donju*: a new class of people, the masters of money who were stealthily transforming the country from a socialist utopia into something whose true nature was still emerging. Surrounded by these nouveau riche types, Jun-su felt nervous. His collar seemed to constrict his neck and he found himself fiddling with his chopsticks.

Guk-ju poured them both some Pothonggang beer and smiled at Jun-su's apparent discomfort. "You have a good friend in Su-ok," he said. "She told me great things about you." He leaned forward and lowered his voice. "You have her to thank for getting you out—"

The arrival of the waitress stopped him from finishing his sentence.

Guk-ju had chosen a restaurant that specialized in the cold buckwheat noodles that are considered a Pyongyang specialty. He ordered noodles for both of them and selected a fish to be braised from the tank of live specimens.

"People have the wrong idea about our country," said Guk-ju when the waitress had gone. "Your life can still have a second act. Look at Uncle Jang. I'm telling you, there are changes afoot."

Jang Song-thaek was a member of the country's elite who was married to the Great Leader's daughter, Kim Kyong-hui. He had fallen out of favor and been sent for reeducation a number of times, but each time had managed to rehabilitate himself. Now his star seemed to be on the rise again. People whispered that he had taken the reins of power and was behind the economic reforms that were changing the country.

Even though Guk-ju was only a few years older than Jun-su, Jun-su felt obliged to address him respectfully as someone of senior status. At the same time, he felt he understood something that Guk-ju didn't. It was hard to put this understanding into words: it was something to do with his memory of hunger, of flesh shrinking in the cold, of emaciated people laying blocks and digging with their bare hands. Jun-su knew that in reality the walls of the restaurant were paper-thin and on the other side were people who would cut your throat for a bowl of cornmeal mush.

"Yesterday Uncle Jang was nothing," said Jun-su quietly.

"Today he may be a general. Tomorrow he may be nothing again."

Guk-ju was silent as he considered Jun-su's words; then he nodded. "You're right, my friend. But people who are useful can be needed for a long time." He took a sip of beer, which left a small mustache of foam. "At least," he added with a self-deprecating smile, "that's my hope." He dabbed the foam off his upper lip. "Now," he said, "I brought you here to talk about your expertise."

"What's my expertise?" said Jun-su.

"The same as mine," said Guk-ju. "Fiction and statistics."

Jun-su got back to the compound in the midafternoon. Jimi was sitting on the sofa in his pajamas watching the film of a rock concert on a screen that took up a whole wall. A cigarette lay in an ashtray on the glass table in front of him, its thin thread of smoke curling upwards.

He muted the sound of the television when he saw Jun-su in his suit.

"Come here," he said. "I want to ask you something."

Jun-su obeyed. He approached, but didn't sit down. On the screen were some leathery old European men playing guitars and pulling faces as they sang into microphones.

"Su-ok told me that you went out with each other at university." Jimi picked up the cigarette and took a drag. When he spoke again, his voice sounded lower and more intimidating. "She claims you never slept together. Is that true? I don't care either way. I just want to know the truth."

"That's the truth," said Jun-su.

Jimi looked both relieved and contemptuous. "She said you were away for a lot of years."

"That's also true."

"Sit down. I'll get the maid to bring you something to drink. What will you have?" He pressed a button that brought one of the Vietnamese attendants scurrying from the kitchen.

"Maybe some tea."

"Tea!" Jimi shook his head scornfully. "Get my little brother here some vodka," he told the maid.

A few minutes later, the maid brought in a silver tray. On it was a bottle of vodka that was blurry with ice crystals and wrapped in a pristine white napkin. Beside it were two shot glasses, some cucumber, some raw fatty tuna, and a dish of orange salmon eggs.

Jimi became animated at the sight of the vodka, but he only poured a glass for Jun-su. "I've got to watch my intake," he said.

Jun-su felt awkward. It seemed strange to be the only one drinking, but he didn't have much of a choice. Jimi was urging him on.

"Long life," said Jun-su, and knocked back the vodka. Jimi refilled Jun-su's glass twice and watched him eagerly as he drank. Jun-su felt his face redden. "It's strong!" he said. "I'm not much of a drinker."

Jimi tutted. "What kind of Korean are you? You don't drink and you claim you didn't sleep with Su-ok."

"I really didn't," insisted Jun-su.

"I believe you, little brother," said Jimi. His eyes strayed to the vodka bottle. "I'll just have one to keep you company."

Jimi drank two shots, one after the other, interspersed with mouthfuls of salmon eggs. He ate greedily, with no self-consciousness. Jun-su envied him. However drunk he got, Jun-su would never be able to occupy his physical space with Jimi's carefree sense of entitlement. Even after leaving the camp, he still felt as though something in him was always either standing to attention or cringing from the threat of a blow.

"Why do they call you Jimi?" Jun-su asked.

Jimi's mouth was full of salmon eggs. He swallowed them down. "Because of Hendrix," he said.

"Forgive my ignorance. I don't know who he is."

"*Forgive my ignorance*. Don't talk to me like I'm your boss. Your punishment for that is more vodka." Jimi refilled Jun-su's shot glass and kept an eye on him to make sure he downed it in one.

"Jimi Hendrix was the greatest guitarist who ever lived." Jimi refilled both glasses. The vodka bottle was now two-thirds empty. "I'm not even close to one-tenth of his talent, but what do they say?" Jimi held up his shot glass in a toast. "You have to aim for the stars to hit the moon."

They both emptied their drinks.

Jimi reached for his acoustic guitar and put it on his lap. He brushed it lightly with his fingers and began playing soft arpeggiated chords. The sounds were sweet and touched with sadness. It felt to Jun-su as though Jimi was putting aside his superficial brashness and cruelty and revealing a more tender side to his character. It made Jun-su want to share something of himself.

"I met your father once," said Jun-su, wiping his mouth with the back of his hand. Jimi glanced up from the guitar. His expression of curiosity encouraged Jun-su to tell the story. "I won a regional poetry competition when I was fifteen," he said. "My teacher and I came to Pyongyang for the finals."

The alcohol had relaxed Jun-su. He enjoyed recounting his visit to the capital, how he'd stood backstage at the theater, how he'd met the Dear Leader, Jimi's father, and been overcome with emotion. He almost mentioned meeting Su-ok, but thought better of it. He capped the anecdote with the Dear Leader's unforgettable line: "You honored me with a poem about my birthplace. It's enough!" It somehow captured the essence of the Dear Leader: innocence and approachability.

"My dad wasn't born on Mount Paektu," said Jimi, leaning forward across the guitar and refilling the shot glasses. "You know that, right?"

"No," said Jun-su.

"He was born in Russia when my grandfather was living there. Mount Paektu is—it's not exactly a lie. It's part of a higher truth." Jimi strummed the guitar and sang a few bars of a song in English. "Do you think Mick Jagger really was born in a *crossfire hurricane*?"

"A metaphor?" suggested Jun-su, though he had no idea what Jimi was talking about.

"Exactly!" Jimi drained his glass and carried on talking. "The Korean people are innocent. They're like children who need to be protected. There are things it's better they're not told yet. Like, you know who started the war, right?"

"Of course," said Jun-su. "The Yankee bastards."

Jimi smirked and wagged his forefinger. "No. We did!"

"We were invaded and had to respond," Jun-su protested.

"No, little brother. Would the Yankee bastards have attacked one day? Probably. But my grandfather started that war. It was a war of self-defense, but he was the one who began it. Sometimes you have to retaliate first." Jimi sighed. "The world is complicated. The truth is complicated. The leader of this country carries a heavy burden. I watched my father make so many sacrifices. When he got the news that my grandfather had died, you know what he did? He locked himself into his office with a revolver. He came this close to pulling the trigger." Jimi measured a hair's breadth between his thumb and forefinger. "He didn't want it. He knew what it meant: US spy satellites tailing you all day. Not trusting anyone besides your family. Deciding who lives and who dies." Jimi shook his head at the pressure all this entailed. "What *he* wanted was to be a filmmaker. He had a real gift for it. Like, for instance, you're a poet. Imagine if you couldn't do the thing you loved. He had less freedom than a prisoner in one of our jails."

Jun-su felt himself flushing at this comparison, but said nothing. He knew he was drunk and he tried to perch his thoughts on the small dry island of sobriety in his alcohol-flooded brain. As Jimi railed against the burden of leadership and the awfulness of the role, Jun-su felt he was almost too vehement. The speech sounded rehearsed. He was aware that, as the Dear Leader's eldest son, Jimi might have expected to succeed his father. But the leadership had passed instead to his younger brother, the Comrade Marshal, Kim Jong-un.

Jimi rang for the maid. "Bring me my medicine chest," he said.

The maid returned with a small metallic case. Jimi clicked open its shiny locks. "Su-ok's going to be furious with me," he said. "But screw her. We're getting to know each other, right? The fact that you're a poet means you can understand what music means to me."

Jimi was sorting through the contents of his medicine chest. "That's Fatherland Molly," he said, shaking a big bag of pills. "Our chemists make it for export. Even Su-ok likes that, but you need a whole weekend to do it properly. One day I'll take you up to Wonsan and we'll drop some and watch *The Matrix*."

The mention of Wonsan cut through Jun-su's drunkenness. A memory of his mother flashed into his mind. He was eleven years old and lying in his bed. "Once there was a boy called Jun-su," his mother was saying. "He was popular, obedient, loyal, happy, and kind and lived a long life." Jun-su closed his eyes briefly to suppress the pang of heartbreak.

"What's the matter?" said Jimi.

"I'm feeling a bit dizzy."

"This will put you straight, comrade. You'll be clearheaded and ready to do battle with the Yankee bastards." Jimi held up a small piece of mirrored glass with two lines of powder on it and a silver tube. He sniffed one of the lines and rubbed his nostril with his finger. "Your turn," he said.

The drugs burned Jun-su's nose and left a sour taste at the back of his throat. But they not only sobered him up, they made him feel vividly alert.

Jimi was now talking very quickly, moving from one subject to another with great earnestness. One moment, he was talking about Su-ok's father smuggling cocaine in a diplomatic bag from Cuba, the next he was describing a guitar in London he wanted to buy, or the pleasures of surfing in Bali. Jun-su just nodded. He felt thrilled to be here, sharing the confidences of one of the most important men in his country. He had an unmistakable sense that something really significant was just about to happen. But as Jimi kept talking, Jun-su's feeling of optimism dwindled away. He found himself thinking again about his parents.

There was the sound of a car arriving. Jimi put his drugs away. "I don't want Su-ok to see this," he said. "We made a pact."

A few minutes later, Su-ok came in. She quickly took in the evidence of their dissipation and shook her head, but there was a smile on her face.

"We had to celebrate," said Jimi. "Your old boyfriend is a good guy, Su-ok. Look, Jun-su, how beautiful she is. She does important work for the Fatherland, then she comes home and looks after me, the big softhearted effeminate loser brother."

"You're drunk," said Su-ok without rancor. She poured herself a glass of vodka and looked Jimi in the eye. "Long life," she said.

Jimi's hand closed on her wrist and he held her gaze. "I'm drunk, but not that drunk," he said.

Jun-su took this as his cue to leave.

Lying on his bed, he felt the room wheeling about him. He ground his teeth, his mind a welter of confusing images. He kept thinking that if he could somehow get outside the compound and find a bicycle, he would be able to ride all the way to Wonsan to see his parents. He wanted to reassure them that he was all right, that the terrible years of his life had miraculously come to an end, and that from now on the three of them would be able to live well.

# OFFICE 39

Of course, when he woke up, Jun-su didn't cycle to Wonsan, or even attempt to leave the compound. He shuffled downstairs and broke the news to Su-ok that he'd been offered a job. She didn't seem surprised.

"So it was you," he said.

Su-ok drank her espresso. "What do you mean?"

"You asked Guk-ju to find a job for me," said Jun-su.

"I thought that you and Guk-ju would have a lot in common," said Su-ok. "I'm glad I was right." She glanced at her watch, a Swiss one, which encircled her wrist with a delicate bracelet of rose gold.

Jun-su startled her by grabbing her hand. She stared at him in horror. "You're torturing me, Su-ok," he said. "Every night I have to listen to you and that man—"

Su-ok detached herself icily from his grip. "I think you need to conduct self-criticism, comrade. This behavior is not worthy of you." She placed her espresso cup in the spotless sink and walked out to her waiting limousine. Jun-su watched through the picture window as the driver ran round the vehicle to be ready to open the door for her.

Jimi appeared surprisingly early that morning. He was wearing pajama bottoms, but no top. His skin was perfectly smooth, like marble. *Princely* was the word that came to Jun-su's mind. He laughed when he saw Jun-su and slapped him jovially on the back. "How is the head, little brother?" His voice was croaky from the previous night's indulgence. "Ready to start again?"

Jun-su's face must have betrayed his horror at the prospect of another drinking bout.

"I'm joking, little brother!" said Jimi as he put a capsule in the espresso machine. "But we'll make a real Korean of you yet!"

Chuckling to himself, he lit a cigarette and carried his coffee over to his favorite sofa. Overnight, invisible hands had made everything impeccable.

"Guk-ju's offered me a job," said Jun-su.

Jimi gave no answer, so Jun-su walked into the sitting area and said it again.

This time, Jimi looked up. "Cool," he said with perfect indifference, and picked up a guitar.

* * *

Jun-su was eager to start work as soon as possible, not because of the work itself but because he found living in the compound with Jun-su and Su-ok, in spite of all its luxury, oppressive.

The job he'd accepted from Guk-ju came with a modest salary; it also entitled him to a number of perks, including a Chinese-made smartphone for keeping in touch with the office. Best of all, he was given a small apartment in a brand-new development on Future Scientist Street.

It was a tiny studio flat, situated on the building's undesirable twentieth floor. Anyone with any influence made sure to be on the fourth floor or below, as problems with the power supply often put the elevators out of action. Construction work was continuing on the building and dust constantly found its way into Jun-su's room, forming piles under the doorsill that reminded him of Jimi's cocaine. But it was the first space where he felt as safe as he had in his parents' apartment.

The building's other inhabitants were mainly younger government employees. A few elite families were scheduled to move in when the construction was completed. Jun-su wasn't entirely sure who the head of the building's People's Unit was: a number of different people seemed to be sharing the role, with no great conscientiousness. Even the compulsory weekly meetings were relaxed and usually ended up with everyone complaining about the builders.

Jun-su still felt pain about Su-ok, but at least he wasn't confronted with the fact of her loss in the same way. She worked in the same building that he and Guk-ju did, but she was far senior to him and had different responsibilities. Sometimes he would see her sweep through the lobby with her entourage on her way to her offices.

All in all, life would have been pleasant, were it not that Jun-su was haunted by anxiety about his parents.

During that first lunch at the noodle restaurant, Guk-ju had sketched out Jun-su's surprising new duties. Jun-su was now a junior employee in a government department that dealt with the state's insurance claims. All the country's most important businesses were insured against various kinds of disaster by the state's insurers, the Korean National Insurance Corporation. Every factory, farm, hotel, fishing trawler, restaurant, and mining concern was legally obliged to buy annual insurance. The biggest policies were underwritten by insurers overseas, in Munich, London, and Geneva.

Whenever a claim was made, the department that Guk-ju headed had to produce an enormous amount of paperwork to support it. These might include witness statements, drawings, police reports, photographs, and maps. For instance, on Jun-su's first day in the office, he was briefed about a huge claim he would be working on relating to a helicopter crash in the industrial city of Kaesong, close to the border with South Korea.

On the day of the accident, the helicopter had been carrying a pregnant woman to a hospital when mechanical failure caused it to fall out of the sky. The helicopter had plunged into a chemical refinery, which blew up, causing trillions of won of damage and killing dozens of workers, whose families needed to be compensated. Hundreds more people were injured, many of them requiring expensive, long-term medical attention.

This claim was being presented to a famous insurance firm in London that had ended up underwriting the policy. Understandably, their loss adjusters were checking every detail of the accident. The team that Jun-su was now part of had the job of responding to their queries, translating the statements into English, and even providing aerial photographs of the crash site. It was an enormous and important assignment. A payment of tens of millions of dollars depended on their work.

Every person named on the claim required pages of documentation. Jun-su was tasked with finding images for each of the crash victims, however minor their injuries. He collated testimonials from doctors and family members with details about their skin grafts and the physiotherapy they needed. His colleagues gathered pictures that showed the extent of the damage. Others created inventories of the destruction, describing and costing it down to the flat tires and broken windows.

On that first day, Guk-ju invited Jun-su into his office for a brief chat. He told him about the other employees and explained that

Jun-su was one of the most junior members of the department, and that, despite their friendship outside the office, he wouldn't be able to show him any favoritism within it.

Guk-ju's desk sat at one end of the room. Behind him hung portraits of the Dear and Great Leaders. However, at the other end, facing Guk-ju and on the left of the door as you entered, was an oil painting of a garden full of irises. It was a copy of a French masterpiece that had been made by artisans in China. Because the room was full of blue smoke from the cigarettes Guk-ju smoked constantly, it felt almost as though you were looking at the garden through an early morning mist.

"Does that make sense?" Guk-ju asked finally.

Jun-su said that it did.

"Any questions?"

Jun-su hesitated.

"What's on your mind?"

"The pregnant woman," he said.

"Which pregnant woman?"

"The one in the helicopter."

"What's the matter with her?" said Guk-ju, lighting another cigarette.

It was difficult for Jun-su to explain tactfully. The idea that in a country where children fought for food scraps in the garbage, an ordinary woman might get a lift to the hospital in a helicopter because of complications with her pregnancy was, frankly, ludicrous.

"It doesn't seem plausible," he said.

"That's not important," said Guk-ju. "She might have been carrying quintuplets. Perhaps she was barren, but the Fatherland's scientists had finally helped her to conceive. Perhaps her husband was the pilot and he was giving her a ride in the helicopter to fulfill a long-held dream."

"That doesn't make sense. They were on the way to the hospital."

Guk-ju gestured impatiently with his cigarette. "We're not interested in these details. Our job is to invent a world where this took place and document it so carefully that no one can claim it didn't happen. If you were smart, you wouldn't be objecting to the pregnant woman, you'd be coming up with another helicopter or a sunken fishing boat, so we could make the claim even bigger."

Jun-su closed the door. The helicopter, the pregnant woman, the fishing boat, the chemical refinery, the dead and injured workers, and their grieving relatives were all, of course, imaginary. It was the job of Jun-su and his new colleagues to make them real.

Almost everyone in North Korea who used a computer was confined to a regulated intranet, a kind of walled garden that excluded traffic from the outside world. In order to do his work, Jun-su was given access to the infinite expanse of the open internet.

There was a daylong orientation for the new users, of whom there were about a dozen. Various departments were expanding as the government sought to generate fresh sources of foreign cash. The most successful of these was the one where Su-ok worked, on the twelfth floor of the building. From this office, computer experts mounted cyberattacks on systems outside the country. They would install ransomware and demand payment to return things to normal. It was extremely lucrative: most foreign companies were happy to pay up in order to avoid the bad publicity that came with the revelation that they'd been hacked.

In the first hour of the orientation, the tutor, a woman in her forties wearing a lot of makeup and a traditional long pink bell-shaped dress, showed her new students a selection of the most disgusting images that could be found on the internet.

Jun-su's new colleagues made audible groans. Some wriggled theatrically in their seats to show their disgust at the material. There was video footage of white men sodomizing an animal, an African pleading as he had his ear cut off, a beheading, two apparently Russian youths beating an Asian man to death, jeering crowds in masks setting someone on fire, other young people attacking elderly passersby and laughing as they did so.

It seemed the tutor's outfit, expressionless made-up face, and low voice had been chosen to heighten the contrast with the hellish on-screen images that she was displaying to the class.

"This is a human sewer in the brain of our enemies," said the tutor. "Tell me something about a sewer: Should you eat out of a sewer?" She paused for dramatic effect. "That's right, you should not."

The message of the orientation was simple: engaging with the outside world through the internet was a disgusting and harmful practice that should only be attempted with caution by those who were fighting on behalf of the Fatherland. Colleagues were urged to monitor each other's intake of this dangerous material and watch for the telltale signs of moral taint. All email addresses were to be held in common. No one would have any secrets from anyone else. There would be special self-criticism and additional political study sessions that were obligatory for anyone with open internet privileges.

Jun-su was careful to speak up at the self-criticism sessions. He confessed to the disturbing feelings that working on the internet aroused, without ever incriminating himself by admitting to anything serious. Whenever in doubt, you could always rely on a few tactical bits of self-reproach. "I haven't worked hard enough to uphold the party line" was the most useful. He could tell that his new colleagues were curious about him, about the strange gaps in his biography and the nature of his relationship to Guk-ju. He made sure to come across as affable, bland, polite, and deeply loyal.

However, he hadn't forgotten the pact he'd made with the fox in the woods above the sanatorium. He learned how to remove cookies from his web browser and he made cautious forays into forbidden corners of the internet. The power of typing something into a search engine and being rewarded with an instantaneous answer seemed like magic from the House of Possibility. No wonder the country's leaders feared giving this ability to its citizens.

The question of Jun-su's true feelings about the system is one that I've often pondered. As a sensitive and intelligent person who had experienced firsthand the cruelty and fanaticism of the North Korean regime, he had every reason to loathe its leadership. No one was in a better position to understand how it took the highest human ideals of loyalty, altruism, and compassion and hitched them to a utopian fantasy that turned them into their opposites. At the same time, he found it infuriating to see his homeland portrayed as a nation of joyless robots. Sometimes he could even find it in his heart to express a certain admiration for the tenacity of its leaders.

The adult Jun-su was always tempted to give his younger self insights that actually belonged to a later and more disillusioned period of his life. Even in prison, Jun-su hadn't let go of the fantasy that the Dear Leader was a loving parent who cared for him. He would tell himself that if Kim Jong-il knew what had befallen the youthful poet whose verses he had praised, he would be outraged and rehabilitate him immediately. The truth is that Jun-su, like all of us, was only ever briefly unitary. He was cohabited by multiple selves, one of whom was eternally a ten-year-old boy in a red neckerchief singing the verses to “My Dear Party, You’re My Mother” at the top of his voice.

The Pyongyang to which Jun-su had returned was very different from the city he remembered. It had changed in his absence, grown richer, more colorful and dissolute.

Its people were noticeably better-fed—a few were even fat. The electricity supply, while still erratic, was much less unreliable. Many citizens now had solar panels on their balconies to charge batteries for use during blackouts. More restaurants had appeared. Informal markets operated openly and kiosks had sprung up throughout the city, selling all sorts of goods—sweets, batteries, cigarettes, fizzy drinks—many of them produced by new North Korean businesses. There were more cars on the streets and more citizens with mobile phones. And in quiet corners of the city, there was also evidence of prostitution and drug abuse.

One night in June, after a long day in the office, Jun-su was walking back to his apartment when he was accosted by a skinny woman. Her age was hard to estimate. Her rotten brown teeth and wrinkled skin marked her out as a user of *bingdu*, a powerful methamphetamine that was illegal but increasingly popular. It suppressed hunger pangs and gave the user a sense of euphoria and energy. It was also highly addictive.

"Hey, comrade," said the woman, "it's your lucky day." Jun-su was shocked by her bold approach and the harshness of her raddled voice. She opened her coat and placed something on the ground. "My last one. A thousand won and it's yours."

Jun-su looked at the object: it was a small fluffy animal. His first thought was that it was a rabbit that the addict had stolen from one of the nearby apartments. Periodically, government campaigns encouraged citizens to raise them for their meat and pelts.

The animal approached him with a knock-kneed gait that made its belly sway from side to side. Jun-su now saw that it was a tiny kitten with milky-green eyes and thin, translucent black fur. It didn't resist when he picked it up. It was the weight of a pair of socks and its stomach was tight and round as though it had swallowed an apricot.

"It likes you," said the addict. "I like your face too, so let's say eight hundred won. It's up to you whether you keep it as a pet or line gloves with it."

Jun-su told himself off for being a softhearted fool, but he pressed the money into the woman's hand.

"In camp, I would have eaten you," he said to the kitten as he carried her home. Her pink mouth opened and closed as she mewed at him plaintively. He wasn't sure whether she was pleading or chastising.

For a reason that he could never fully explain, he decided to give her an English name. He called her Cat.

Jun-su took Cat up to his apartment in his jacket pocket. He opened a tin of sprats and fed her from his hand. Then she fell asleep, her tiny belly rising and falling. He let her sleep on his mattress and, having removed all the photos and bold print references to the Supreme Leader, he tore up some newspaper and made a pile of it for her to shit in.

A month after starting his job and two weeks after finding Cat, Jun-su got up at dawn one Sunday and caught an intercity bus to Wonsan. It was packed, and stopped frequently at the checkpoints at the city limits, but it was still faster than the train.

On board, Jun-su was astonished to see how many people were using mobile phones. These were ordinary people, not the elite. It was a reminder to him how much had changed since his incarceration. It filled him with a sense of optimism. Perhaps Uncle Jang really was beginning to change the country for the better.

Around noon the bus pulled into Wonsan, and Jun-su walked the three kilometers to his parents' apartment.

There was no one in the glass booth on the ground floor, so Jun-su climbed the stairs.

From the corridor, he could hear the sound of a baby crying in his old apartment. He rapped on the door and it was opened by a young man about his own age, who was wearing a stained undershirt. "Hello, comrade," said Jun-su. "I'm looking for the people who used to live here."

The man scratched his head and called for his wife. She was breastfeeding a child while a weeping toddler trailed after her.

"We moved in last year," said the woman. "Why don't you ask the head of the building committee?"

"There was no one down there," said Jun-su. "Who is in charge now?"

"It's Mrs. Kim. She's probably in her apartment."

"Mrs. Kim with the . . . ?" Jun-su mimed the distinctive back-combed hairstyle that he remembered the old superintendent wearing.

The couple both smiled. "That one," said the man.

Mrs. Kim opened her door slowly and peered out. Everything about her was thinner and grayer, but her beady eyes shone with undiminished malevolence. "Ah," she said, catching sight of Jun-su. "It's the enemy of the people! So they let you live." She tutted with disapproval.

"I'm looking for my parents," said Jun-su.

"They moved," said Mrs. Kim. "It should have happened sooner. They didn't need all that space."

"Do you have an address for them?" he asked.

"Wait there," said Mrs. Kim. She pushed the door to and went back inside. A few minutes later, she emerged holding a piece of paper. It said *Hospital 49* in pencil and it gave a mailing address near Changrim, a small town roughly equidistant between Wonsan and Pyongyang. "Here," she said. "Tell your mother she still owes me fifty won for the cleaning. They left the apartment in a terrible mess."

"Fifty won, you say?" Jun-su reached into his pocket and drew out a note. "That makes us quits, Mrs. Kim."

Mrs. Kim took the offered note and closed the door.

As Jun-su traveled back to Pyongyang, rain was hammering the fields. Just beyond the road, two men wearing plastic bin bags were trying to move a cart that had become mud-bound. Mrs. Kim's words preyed on Jun-su's mind.

The term *Hospital 49* was familiar to him, as it was to his fellow citizens. There were Hospital 49s around the country, mostly tucked away in rural areas. They were psychiatric institutions and almost no one had any idea what went on inside them.

A few hundred meters from Jun-su's office, a new Italian restaurant had opened. Pizza chefs had come from Italy to train its staff to use the imported Italian pizza ovens. There was also a stage at the rear of the restaurant where female performers sang patriotic songs to the backing of a karaoke machine.

When the work on the helicopter claim was finally completed and dispatched to London, Guk-ju treated his whole team of a dozen people to a meal there. They toasted each other in beer and soju and the mood grew rowdy.

Guk-ju's face had turned red and blotchy from the alcohol. He clapped an arm round Jun-su's shoulders and breathed soju fumes into his ear. "I have another big project coming up," he said in a conspiratorial voice. "I can't let you into the details yet, but it involves a rocket."

Jun-su decided this was the opportunity he'd been waiting for. He lowered his voice. "Listen, brother, I have a favor to ask. You know my situation. I haven't seen my parents for ten years. I don't think they even know I'm alive. Can you get me a travel pass so I can visit them?"

Guk-ju scrunched up his drunken face and dismissed Jun-su's request with a wave of his hand. "But you don't need a pass. You can go to Wonsan with your government ID."

"They're not in Wonsan anymore," said Jun-su. "They're near Changrim. In a Hospital Forty-Nine."

At the mention of the hospital, Guk-ju grew cautious. "That's more complicated," he said. "I'll have to have a word with Su-ok about this."

The official salary for Jun-su's new job was small. However, the rations he was entitled to from the state distribution center arrived on time and were of excellent quality. In addition to this, every month he received an additional pay packet in dollar bills: two hundred of them a month—a fortune. At first Jun-su had resisted the temptation to spend it. He wanted to save his money so he had something to give his parents when he saw them. But after the trip to Wonsan, he had splashed out on a Chinese-made television set that connected to an aerial socket in his apartment and received the three state channels: Central Korean TV, Educational TV, and Mansudae TV. The television was one of the few possessions in his tiny unfurnished flat.

After the news at eight o'clock, Jun-su liked watching a comedy show called *Take a Look* that had been broadcast regularly since the seventies.

In fact, nothing about the program was very funny. The performers were usually a man and a woman in military uniform who had surreal conversations with one another. They shared the kind of naïve and meaningless banter that six-year-olds might indulge in: whimsical riffs about food, absent-minded relatives, and visits to the beach. The show was always sure to conclude with heartfelt declarations of loyalty to the regime. All the same, there was something about its familiarity and innocence that felt consoling.

Tonight, however, *Take a Look* wasn't on. Mansudae TV was about to show a film from Jun-su's childhood: *O Youth!*, a romantic comedy that told the story of a young man who falls in love with a female taekwondo instructor. Jun-su remembered watching it as a nine-year-old. His father had taken him to the hotel to watch it on the television in the staff room as a special treat.

Jun-su was just debating whether he had time to pop down to the kiosk to buy a tin of sprats for Cat before it started, when there was a knock at the door.

He dumped Cat in the bathroom and shut her in; pets were against the rules. At a push, he might be able to bribe his visitor to turn a blind eye, but he didn't want to risk it.

Even now, restored to membership of the Workers' Party and as a state employee with high status, Jun-su experienced a surge of anxiety whenever he opened the door to an unfamiliar person. His way of dealing with it was to still his expressive features with a look of modesty and obedience.

He opened the door wearing this invisible mask.

It was Su-ok. "Are you all right?" she said.

"Yes. Why?"

"Your face looks weird."

"Weird how?"

The faint smell of Su-ok's perfume mingled with the building dust. "Can I come in?" she said. "I'd rather not have this conversation in the corridor."

Jun-su moved aside to let her in. She was dressed in one of the dark business outfits that she wore to work: skirt and jacket, a simple white shirt, and flat shoes. Were it not for the portrait of the Great Leader on her lapel, she could have been an ambitious young executive in any country in the world.

"I brought you the paperwork you asked for," said Su-ok. "It was quicker to come myself." She passed him permission slips bearing many official-looking stamps. "And I was curious to see where you're living." She surveyed the bare walls. "It's very Zen."

Jun-su laughed. "That's another word for empty."

The sound of scratching came from the bathroom. Su-ok looked puzzled.

"Let me introduce you to my flatmate," said Jun-su. He cracked open the bathroom door. Cat's face appeared in the gap, looking suspiciously at the visitor. She mewed as Jun-su scooped her up in one hand. "This is Cat." He held her out for Su-ok to stroke.

"Very *kawaii*, as the Japanese say," said Su-ok. She reached across, but instead of stroking the cat, she let her fingers brush Jun-su's jaw. Her touch made his skin tingle. He stood there in shock.

"I can't stay long," she said. "The driver's waiting. If you're going to kiss me, you'd better do it soon."

Jun-su let Cat drop. Her paws landed lightly on the floor as Jun-su's lips met Su-ok's.

Afterwards, Su-ok pulled a sheet around her and they sprawled on the disarranged mattress like lovers with all the time in the world.

"We should be careful what we say," whispered Jun-su.

"There's nothing to worry about for now," said Su-ok.

"There's no listening equipment here. You're freer than I am." She kissed his hands, then stood up and started getting dressed.

Jun-su watched her snapping on her wristwatch and wriggling into her underwear. She turned around and sat down next to him so he could button the neck of her blouse. He kissed her neck and joined his hands around her, under her warm armpits, enveloping her body and squeezing her small breasts, trying to draw her back into bed.

"Don't go," pleaded Jun-su.

She detached herself from him gently and reluctantly, yielding to the pull of the real world.

Now that he had the official travel documents from Su-ok, Jun-su felt able to ask Guk-ju for the use of one of the department's vehicles.

He was assigned an old Russian car, driven by a young soldier who couldn't have been more than twenty.

The soldier tried to make small talk, but Jun-su was keen to keep conversation to a minimum.

Jun-su knew the young soldier must be very well connected to get such a plum job. It was a privilege to be allowed to learn to drive during military service.

They left the highway at Songchon and turned south onto an unpaved road that led through a fertile valley running between the Ahobiryong Mountains. The valley floor was planted with rice.

The driver had to stop and ask for directions from farmworkers. It turned out that the hospital was nowhere near Changrim. It stood on its own at the end of a dirt track, a depressing chunk of stained concrete with dirty windows. There were no murals here. Neither the Great nor the Dear Leader had ever come to offer on-the-spot guidance about the correct approach to treating mental illness.

At first Jun-su didn't even recognize his mother. Her head had been shaved and she was wearing a dirty nightdress. She looked much older than her fifty-five years.

The dormitory smelled of sour milk. A toothless man sat on the end of his ragged mattress trembling.

"Do men and women live in the same room?" Jun-su asked the orderly who showed him in.

"We've had no complaints. Their families understand that the Fatherland must prioritize the needs of productive workers," she said.

Jun-su sat beside his mother and took her hand. It was cold and papery, but something about the touch was still familiar.

"Hello, Mother," he said, using the formal word *eomeoni*. "It's me, Jun-su."

His mother smiled and attempted to stand up from her place on the floor. Jun-su urged her to remain seated. "My son Jun-su is serving in the People's Army," she said loudly. "He must be about your age. He's a big strong boy, like his father, the famous chef. He writes to me every week."

"I am Jun-su," he said. There was not even a glimmer of recognition in her eyes. "Mum," he pleaded, "it's me."

In desperation, Jun-su had switched to the informal word for mother: *eomma*. But Kang Han-na looked affronted and uneasy, as if his plea for intimacy was a lapse of taste and etiquette.

Now she spoke in a whisper. "Be careful what you say about Jun-su. The head of the Regional Party Committee is extremely upset. There were rumors about his son and my cousin Yeong-nam. He said Jun-su should have reported him."

"Reported who?"

Jun-su's mother rocked back and forth indignantly. "Reported who! Pork meat is almost twenty thousand won per kilo now. And they called me a bloodsucker!"

"What happened to my father? What happened to Cho So-dok?"

"Cho So-dok?" At the sound of the name, Jun-su's mother stopped rocking. "My husband was a very good man. Did you know him?"

"Yes," said Jun-su.

"Then you know what I'm talking about." Jun-su's mother stood up and went over to a battered plywood chest of drawers. The top drawer was marked with her surname: *Kang*. She reached in and took out a thin plastic bag that held dried corn kernels. She handed the bag to Jun-su.

"I don't need this. I've eaten," said Jun-su.

His mother's face opened in a gummy smile. He saw with

a pang how she'd let her teeth go. She had always been fastidious about hygiene, boiling up her own homemade soap from mackerel oil and brooking no nonsense when he protested about its weird smell. "Not for you, silly. For the birds."

At his mother's appearance outside the building, a dozen half-tame sparrows and finches descended to peck at the corn kernels she deposited on the concrete path. His mother clucked and chided them with satisfaction.

The orderly, who had followed them out, was standing to one side, observing the scene without interest. Jun-su approached her and gently but firmly grasped her elbow.

"I'm her son. I do very important work in Pyongyang." He flashed the government ID that marked him out as an employee of Office 39. The orderly's eyes widened at this proof of his status. "When I come back next week, I want to see this ward clean and my mother in a private room, otherwise I'm going to take it up with the Regional Party Chairman. Do you understand?"

The orderly nodded fearfully.

"Here." Jun-su pressed a handful of fifty-won notes into her palm to show he wasn't entirely unreasonable.

Su-ok visited Jun-su's apartment again at the end of July.

They turned up the volume of the television set to drown out the sound of their lovemaking.

Afterwards, as they savored the stolen minutes in bed together, Jun-su found himself remembering something Teacher Kang had said many years earlier. "Do you ever wonder if we're good or bad, Su-ok?" he asked.

"We're bad, Jun-su," said Su-ok with a laugh.

"Are you sure? Aren't we the kind of good that breaks rules for a higher kind of goodness?"

"No," said Su-ok, stroking his cheek lightly. "You're rationalizing it. We're the bad that breaks rules for pure pleasure."

"Really?" Jun-su rolled onto his front to look at her. He was quite serious now. "Why me, then? From what I overheard at your house, it sounded like you and Jimi have a lot of pure pleasure."

"I know what you're trying to do, Jun-su," said Su-ok.

"What am I trying to do?"

"You want me to say I love you."

"Do you?" asked Jun-su curiously.

"If you can't already see it, then you're an idiot," said Su-ok.

That weekend, the subject of Jun-su's loud television set was brought up by one of his neighbors at the Daily Life Unity Critique. Jun-su apologized for his thoughtlessness and volunteered to sweep the corridors as a form of expiation.

About a week after he slept with Su-ok for the second time, Jun-su came home late from work to find a car waiting outside his apartment. The driver got out just as Jun-su approached. It was Mr. Shin. "Special orders," said Mr. Shin with a strained smile, holding open the passenger door for Jun-su. It was clear that Jun-su had no choice but to get in.

Jun-su's heart sank. He was on his way back to prison. Soon he would find himself once more in the stinking barracks. How could he have been so reckless as to sleep with Su-ok? Now he was going to pay for it. But as Mr. Shin maneuvered the Mercedes through the empty streets, Jun-su quickly gathered that they were on their way to the compound.

He arrived to find Jimi stretched out on a sofa. On the other side of the room, a tall European was admiring Jimi's collection of guitars. Jimi clicked off the television and stood up. He had gained weight since they had last seen each other and he looked listless. "Thanks for coming, little brother," he said. "There's someone I want you to meet. This is Hans."

The visitor had picked one of the guitars off the wall and turned to Jun-su still holding it. He pronounced a traditional Korean greeting with a thick German accent.

"Hans and I were at school together," said Jimi. "He's visiting from Switzerland."

Jun-su's first impression of Hans was negative. Hans had straight dark hair like a Korean, but his eyes were blue and he had a pronounced beaky nose. There was something shifty and insincere about him. He was deferential to Jimi, but it wasn't the sincere deference of, say, Mr. Shin, who had been raised to regard Jimi and his family as the sacred offspring of the Mount Paektu bloodline. Hans's deference seemed altogether more calculating: he was constantly weighing his words and considering their impact on Jimi.

"I want you to show Hans your game," said Jimi in English.

Jun-su found it disconcerting to hear Jimi speak a foreign language. It stripped away a layer of mystique and revealed him as he was: a spoiled princeling who was used to getting his own way. "I didn't bring my books," said Jun-su.

"I'll send Mr. Shin to get them. Give me your keys." Jimi held out his hand.

Jun-su hesitated.

"Come on, little brother," said Jimi impatiently. "What's the matter?"

Jun-su handed over the keys reluctantly. He had an uncomfortable feeling about surrendering them. Once he was in the flat, what else would Mr. Shin look for? Would he find evidence that Su-ok had been there? Would he bug the apartment? Jun-su was sure his duplicity was transparently obvious. "The thing is," he said, "I've got something in there I shouldn't have."

"What is it, little brother?" Jimi sounded intrigued.

"A cat."

Jimi laughed. "Don't worry. Mr. Shin is good with animals." He tossed the keys to Hans and said something to him in German. Hans left the room.

Once they were alone, Jimi switched back to his native tongue. "Hans is here on business," he explained. "We were supposed to be meeting with my brother, but he kept us waiting for two days and then canceled at the last minute." He looked pensive and sad. "It's complicated being me, little brother," said Jimi wistfully. "Everyone expects me to do things for them, but really, what power do I actually have?"

The plaintive note in his voice struck Jun-su. He had never given much thought to the question of Jimi's internal life. He had always assumed Jimi's unimaginable privilege insulated him from the worries that afflicted normal people. But here he was, like the deputy manager of a provincial factory, fretting over his inability to broker a deal between an ally and his brother, the powerful boss.

When Hans came back, the three of them killed time by drinking cognac until Mr. Shin returned with the dice and the rule books. The alcohol made Hans more unguarded. He kept returning to the subject of his wasted trip, something to do with a joint venture in a copper mining concern. At one point, Jun-su heard Hans say in English, "Your brother is such a douche." Jimi gave him a hard stare, and Hans lowered his eyes and muttered something in German.

The three of them didn't start playing until past ten o'clock. Jun-su decided to play a simple dungeon crawl that had pregenerated characters and was included with one of the new rule books. It was a fairly challenging adventure—some of the monsters were dangerously strong and could overwhelm a tiny party of two adventurers. So in addition to Hans's dwarf fighter, Gimli, and Jimi's bard, Eric, Jun-su bolstered their team with a non-player character: an elf magician called Dolores Silverbow.

They played for about an hour. With Dolores's help, they were able to enter the dungeon and make quite good progress. Hans rolled a joint which, at Jimi's insistence, Jun-su smoked a little of. He found the cannabis made his mind feel light and agile. It also seemed to increase his sensitivity to his environment. He could see stress and anxiety looming over Jimi like a dark cloud. And he could sense the disappointment and frustration that had built up in Hans during his wasted trip to Pyongyang.

Things came to a head when Hans's character slipped into a trap filled with quicksand. Jun-su passed Hans the twenty-sided die. "You need a twelve or bigger to get out," he said.

Hans rolled a one. "Under the rules we play, that's a hard fail," said Jun-su. "You feel the sand closing over your nose and mouth. The weight of it crushes your chest. As you struggle to breathe, the sand forces itself down your throat and into your lungs. You black out."

It was clear that Hans was very annoyed to have died—and that Jimi was rather pleased to have seen him off. "*Sayonara*, Gimli," said Jimi. "Now it's just me and the hot NPC riding off into the sunset."

After the cognac, the marijuana, and the wasted trip, Gimli's unexpected death was the last straw. Hans looked murderously disappointed. "You're the goddamn NPC, Jimi!" he said, in what must have been an attempt at humor.

A dark look came over Jimi's face. Jun-su could see that Hans had hit a nerve. In fact, he could hardly have said a more wounding sentence. Jimi stared silently at Hans, tight-lipped and furious. Seconds ticked by. Jimi's exaggerated reaction was compounding the disaster. He might have chosen to brush off Hans's words as a foolish remark, but he seemed determined to magnify the insult and impale himself on it. It was as though something in him relished the exposure of his private shame.

"I'm kidding, man," said Hans, which just made everything worse. "Don't take everything so serious."

Without another word, Jimi got up and left the room.

"Shit, man. What did I say?" said Hans, turning to Jun-su. "He had a major sense of humor failure."

Jun-su began packing up the game.

"What? You leaving too?"

"You're dead and I've got work in the morning," said Jun-su.

"This whole thing's been a bust," said Hans. "This is so not what I was promised." He lay back on the couch, slurping his cognac disconsolately out of the tumbler.

Mr. Shin drove Jun-su back to his apartment in silence. There had been a power outage and the warm night was as deep and black as a pot of ink.

* * *

As Pyongyang sweltered in a summer heat wave, Jun-su found himself spending longer and longer hours at work. His department was trying to coax the big insurance claim through the sluggish bureaucracy of the British underwriters.

Every day the fax machine in his office belched out pages of queries from London. The British insurers were doing their utmost to reduce the amount of the payment. They were unhappy about both its size and the fact that they couldn't send their own loss adjusters to verify the claim in person.

"This was always part of the arrangement," tutted Guk-ju. "They knew what they were getting into. They'll make a fuss for a while, then they'll have to agree. They're still accepting our premiums for other policies."

As soon as the problems had arisen, Jun-su had volunteered to help. He understood that he owed his place in this world to the patronage of Su-ok. Now he wanted to earn the respect of Guk-ju and secure his position—for the sake of his mother, if not himself.

He threw himself into the project wholeheartedly, with the same attention to detail that he put into running an adventure in the House of Possibility. He made a point of knowing everything about the invented world, from the engineering specifications of the crashed aircraft to the biographies of its passengers. As the case drew on, Guk-ju started to take note of Jun-su's efforts. If he hadn't already seen it, he now began to appreciate the potential of his newest colleague.

The department was under pressure to secure the money. They had started working seven days a week. It was part of a bigger push that was made clear to them at their biweekly political meetings. In fact, the rationale behind their frantic work schedule resembled nothing so much as a story from one of Jun-su's old comic books.

In 2009, the late Dear Leader had finally announced the successful test of a nuclear weapon. In response, the outside world, duped by the hypocrites of the United States, had imposed economic sanctions. The whole country was suffering.

As an embargo choked the Korean people, the government needed to find other ways to generate cash. The priority was to fund the military. Without a strong army to protect them, the people would be vulnerable to the Yankee warmongers, whose ultimate goal was to reduce them to a state of lackeydom.

There were many ways for people to earn hard currency for the war effort. Some well-connected citizens had been granted licenses to open restaurants in China; they sent back a big portion of the receipts to the government. Brigades of North Korean men had been hired out to work in logging camps in the vast softwood forests of Siberia. The country's chemists were producing amphetamines in state-run laboratories for export across Asia. Su-ok's department had refined computer hacking to a virtual art form. No system in the world was safe from the country's ransomware. And Guk-ju's ingenious insurance scams were on the brink of generating millions of dollars.

The doctrine that made such devious practices not only possible but desirable was one that Jun-su had imbibed since birth. Koreans were a special race, the holy offspring of the mythical god-king Tangun. Only in North Korea had their historic specialness been preserved by the efforts of the Kim Dynasty. The unique quality of the Korean race was pure-hearted innocence. Childlike, gentle, and spontaneous, they were constantly at risk from the outside world. Over centuries, this identity had come under attack many times, but suffering had only tempered it like metal, making it purer and sweeter. The Korean people needed the protection and guidance of the Workers' Party on one hand and the Kim dynasty on the other. Only under their special care would the children of North Korea be loved and safe enough to fulfill their historic destiny.

In late August, Jun-su took a weekend off work to leave the city again. This time he went back to Wonsan.

At the Songdowon Hotel, he entered the familiar lobby and asked a receptionist if he knew of any way to contact a former employee called Cho So-dok.

"Former employee?" said the receptionist with puzzlement. "The only Cho So-dok I know is the head chef."

So-dok was in his chef's whites, smoking out on the balcony before he went back to discuss the preparation of a wedding banquet with a local dignitary.

As they embraced, Jun-su felt his father's bony shoulder blades. His dad's ineffable scent and the smells of garlic and cigarette smoke drew tears from Jun-su's eyes.

The blue-gray water of the East Sea was very still, faintly wrinkled by a soft breeze. In the distance, the strange ziggurats of new hotels under construction were visible on the waterfront. They were being built to house the hordes of foreign tourists that the government wanted to draw to Wonsan as another source of foreign money.

"I heard a rumor that you were back from the mountains," said So-dok. "Let me look at you. You look well. You're handsome! A chip off the old block."

"A friend helped me find work in the capital," said Jun-su. "Things are good."

So-dok smiled as he gazed at his son. "Are you free to have dinner with me? Come tonight. I want you to meet someone."

Jun-su killed time walking along the seafront and turned up at his father's apartment before seven. The door was opened by a shy-looking woman in her fifties.

She introduced herself as Bok-mi. "I've known your father for years," she said. The name echoed distantly in Jun-su's mind. This matronly woman bore no resemblance to the young chambermaid he'd envisaged peering beneath a bed and discovering the book that had become part of his destiny.

"We need to celebrate your freedom and your new job," said So-dok, handing Jun-su a cup of soju.

Bok-mi was very solicitous and brought plate after plate of food from the kitchen while So-dok and Jun-su drank and chatted. But the atmosphere of celebration felt false. Jun-su was disturbed by his father's complacency, the presence of this strange woman, and his recollection of his mother, shorn of her hair, in the stinking hospital.

"What happened to you and Mum?" said Jun-su, when Bok-mi was in the kitchen fetching some snacks.

So-dok finished his drink, grimaced, and wiped his mouth. "There were things about your mother's family I never told you," he said. "We started living apart once you went to university. Your arrest was the final straw. Besides, a whole lifetime is too long to spend with someone you don't love."

"Don't love? What are you talking about?" protested Jun-su.

"I'm speaking to you man-to-man here. I met Bok-mi at work. I didn't want to hurt your mother, but love is love."

So-dok fell silent as Bok-mi entered the room with a plate of fried zucchini. He resumed speaking after she went back to the kitchen. "When the divorce came through, she went to work in a garment factory in Kaesong. I'm sorry to hear she's not well in the head. But I'm not surprised. The whole family had mental problems. Like that old pervert Kang."

"Teacher Kang?"

"Yes, the one who caused you all the trouble with his crazy

game. Her cousin on her dad's side. We should never have let him into the house." So-dok shook his head and rubbed his chin regretfully.

That night Jun-su unrolled a mattress in his father's living room and lay down to sleep. The smell of fried food still hung in the air, so he opened the windows to freshen the atmosphere. As the curtains parted, a shaft of moonlight fell upon the joint portraits of the Great Leader and the Dear Leader. Under their loving gazes, Jun-su fell asleep and dreamed he was suffocating to death in quicksand.

The next morning, Jun-su's head ached from his father's soju. Bok-mi made them a traditional hangover cure for breakfast: a pickled cabbage fritter and egg soup.

So-dok was due at work for a political study session. He and Jun-su walked together as far as the bus station.

On the way, Jun-su's phone began to ring. The only person who ever called him was Guk-ju, always with a question about work. But this time, the display didn't show Guk-ju's number.

"Hey, little brother," said the caller. It was Jimi. His voice sounded hoarse. "I'm hearing a rumor that you're in Wonsan. Stay where you are and I'll send a car for you."

"Who is it?" said So-dok, after he'd hung up.

"A friend of mine is here for work," said Jun-su. "I'm going to see him before I go back to the capital. Let's say farewell here."

Jun-su embraced his father. After they'd said good-bye, Jun-su watched him walk along the curving seafront road to the hotel. Even at a distance of a hundred meters, there was still something about his father's walk that made it distinctly his. Jun-su felt he would have recognized it anywhere: the unique Cho-So-dok-ness of his gait. But what it was *precisely* was difficult to say. And then an army vehicle blocked his line of sight for an instant, and when it had passed, his father had vanished into the crowd.

A Mercedes took Jun-su to a walled compound on the seafront. At the entrance, he was searched for weapons and then transferred to a golf cart driven by a member of the Supreme Guard Command, the elite bodyguards charged with defending the lives of the ruling family.

The golf cart turned off the main avenue and up a narrow path into a thicket of trees. Less than a kilometer farther on, it parked outside a rustic-looking shack thatched with palm leaves and surrounded by carved timber posts.

Jimi emerged looking haggard and wearing a half-open dressing gown. He dismissed the driver with a gesture. The driver reversed expertly back down the narrow path.

"I call this my Robinson Crusoe hut, little brother," said Jimi. "Come inside. This was one of my father's favorite places. We'd come here and pretend to be shipwrecked."

The interior had an indefinable aesthetic: it was like a Polynesian hut that had been decorated with medieval European artifacts. It turned out to have been part of an old film set that had been dismantled and reconstructed here at the whim of the Dear Leader.

"They used to use this for themed parties. My dad told me that once the whole politburo dressed up in grass skirts and drank Hennessy out of coconuts," said Jimi. "And he was giving me the family-friendly version. You know about the Pleasure Brigade? These walls have seen some crazy shit." An acoustic guitar lay on a bench that had been fashioned from a single tree trunk. There were trays of half-eaten food stacked in a corner of the sitting area. "I've been writing some songs for my album," Jimi added by way of explanation. "I'm thinking about booking some studio time at a friend's place in Manila."

Piles of white powder lay on a low table. Jimi spooned some into his nostrils. He took an orange pill bottle out of his pocket, swallowed a handful of tablets, and washed them down with a swig of cognac from an open bottle. The drugs visibly enlivened him; his eyes had a wild, distracted look. "What are you doing in Wonsan, little brother?" he asked.

Jun-su explained that he had been visiting his father, but it was clear that Jimi was too preoccupied with his own disordered thoughts to listen. He laid the guitar over his lap and strummed it discordantly.

"Tell me something, little brother," said Jimi, "and tell me honestly. Do you think I'm an NPC?" There was a strange combination of vulnerability and defensiveness in the way he posed the question.

Jun-su hesitated, and before he could open his mouth, Jimi had interrupted.

"Actually, don't answer. I know you'll deny it," Jimi said, shaking his head. He took a flick-knife from his pocket, sprang the blade, and began scraping the heaps of white powder into neat lines. "Want one?"

Jun-su shook his head.

Instead of strong-arming him into another dissipation, Jimi simply accepted Jun-su's refusal. It was further evidence of his depressed state of mind. He snorted some drugs from the table and lay back against a cushion in a reflective mood. "You know, when I was at school in Switzerland, I had a pretty ordinary life. I got average grades and worried about hooking up with girls and having the latest sneakers. Regular teenage stuff, right?"

Jun-su nodded, but he was thinking how far that was from the preoccupations of his own teenage years, when he was memorizing the life stories of Jimi's father and grandfather and learning to castigate himself at the Daily Life Unity Critique for insufficient revolutionary zeal.

"So that was one life." Jimi scooped another of the lines onto his knife and inhaled it directly from the blade. "Then in the vacations, we'd come back home and as soon as the plane landed, it was like we were in another world. From Switzerland, it didn't seem like it could be real. It was like Hogwarts, or that movie where there's a fairyland at the back of a cupboard. But sure enough, we'd arrive in a world where my mum and dad were king and queen and I was a king-in-waiting. My dad would come here—he'd sit just where you're sitting now, and he'd complain about his work and he'd ask my advice about how to run the country. You know, it was supposed to be my destiny to follow him. And now I'm sitting here in a dressing gown and the Workers' Party is discussing putting my younger brother on a badge, which you and I are going to have to wear. It's like there have only been three real people in the history of this country: my grandfather, my dad, and my younger brother. I mean, what's going on? It was only a few years ago they were going to put *me* on a badge. I was supposed to be the leader. But people said I was soft and weak."

"I thought you didn't want to be leader," said Jun-su.

"That's not the point!" said Jimi. "It's not fair. It was my birthright. Now I'm like everyone else: I'm not real. I'm an NPC." He turned to Jun-su and added viciously, "And so are you."

"I'm not an NPC," said Jun-su. "I'm real."

"How do you know?" said Jimi, clearly annoyed by Jun-su's answer. "You have no power, none. My brother could put you back in a prison camp tomorrow. Everything you have can be taken away. What makes you think you're real?"

The buzz of a chain saw came from a distant part of the compound. It was far enough away to sound almost soothing. A team of gardeners was landscaping the property. And yet barely a stone's throw from these walls, Jun-su thought, other people were digging potatoes with their hands, and coaxing bullocks into a harness, and going without food, and betraying their friends. But here, in this enclave of luxury, shapely trees were being pruned with the best Japanese or German machinery.

*I learned who I was in one of your father's prisons*, Jun-su wanted to say. But he saw the alert amber eyes of the fox warning him to be prudent.

"If anyone's an NPC, it's your brother," said Jun-su. "He's like an actor in a play. He can choose from a handful of different lines, but all his parts are written for him by other people."

Jun-su knew this was blasphemous talk. It would certainly result in death if anyone overheard it. But he could also see that his words had pleased Jimi. He went on: "You're bringing yourself down. You need to get out of this place. This isn't helping you, being in here and brooding. Come outside."

Jimi followed Jun-su onto the veranda and stood there, his pale belly visible through the flaps of his dressing gown, eyes blinking in the sunlight. "What do you know, little brother?" said Jimi softly. "You're a good talker, but these are just words."

Jun-su looked him in the eye. "You think Su-ok would be with someone she thought was an NPC?"

Jimi stared up at the sky and rubbed his hand down his face as though he wanted to wipe off its pained expression. He suddenly looked both relieved and tearful. He put his arms round Jun-su. His rank, unwashed smell made Jun-su think of decaying fruit. "Thanks, little brother," said Jimi. "I won't forget this."

Jun-su stayed for another hour while Jimi got dressed, and then they traveled back to the capital together. Jimi took a handful of tranquilizers to cope with the comedown and was dazed and unresponsive throughout the drive.

It was strange to think that this swift, efficient journey of a few hours down an empty highway was the same one that had once taken Jun-su and Teacher Mun the best part of a day. In Jimi's Mercedes, with its special license plates and Mr. Shin at the wheel, time became compressed. Yet outside the car, the normal rules of life applied. Jun-su saw people squatting in the road, waiting for the irregular buses or the transport that might eventually be sent from their collective farms. How much of their lives was spent in waiting! Waiting for the bus, waiting for their day to collect rations from the distribution center, waiting for a glimpse of the leader, waiting for on-the-spot guidance, waiting for the decisive arrival of socialism that would finally make sense of all their waiting.

A week later, just after sunrise, the young soldier who had previously driven Jun-su to Changrim arrived at the apartment block on Future Scientist Street. The strains of "Where Are You, Dear General?" had been playing from the city's loudspeakers since 5 a.m. As he got into the car and they drove off, Jun-su lowered the windows to hear it better.

The song's melancholy cadences drifted over the empty streets every morning. Its lyrics were about longing for the guidance of the country's spiritual father, Kim Il-sung. "Where is the fatherly General, when the Big Dipper lights the sky? Where are the light-flooded windows of his Supreme Headquarters?" Even in this, its instrumental version, distorted by the amplifiers through which it was broadcast, the tune conveyed a feeling of transcendent heartache. Like the best sacred music, it possessed a yearning quality, evoking a wish to be released from earthly worries and reunited with a caring and omnipotent parent. It never failed to move Jun-su and make him miss his family. And today, at least, he was on his way to see his mother.

They reached the hospital around midday. Han-na had been relocated, as he had asked, to a room of her own.

"Hello, comrade," she said brightly as he came in.

"I want you to know something," he said. "I spoke to Jun-su."

"My son Jun-su? How is he? That scamp. I expect he's too busy to write."

"He wrote you a letter," said Jun-su. "It's here."

Jun-su put it in her hand. He had poured into it everything he felt for her: his love and gratitude, his regret at the breakup of his parents' marriage, and he explained that he had space for her in his apartment in Pyongyang and would like her to move there. She read his words without emotion.

"He wants you to come live with him," said Jun-su. "He has a big apartment."

Han-na wrinkled up her nose and put the letter down. "What would I do in Pyongyang?" she said. "I'm a provincial girl."

"You can do whatever you want," said Jun-su. "There are parks and museums."

"I'm needed here," said Han-na, sounding suddenly anxious. "I'm extremely busy. Who else is going to feed the birds? Besides, I'm working on a book about my life and my love for the Dear Leader."

They sat in silence for a while. His mother was the first to speak.

"Are you going to see Jun-su?" she said.

"*Eomma*," he said, "I am Jun-su."

"Stop being stupid: Are you going to see him or not?"

"Yes," said Jun-su sadly.

"Good. I have a few things that I've been meaning to give him." Han-na indicated a battered cardboard suitcase in the corner of the room. At her request, Jun-su opened it.

It was full of papers: school reports, notes from old self-criticism sessions. Inside a thick envelope bearing the stamp of the Ministry of State Security was a letter informing Jun-su's parents that their son had been selected for rerevolutionizing.

Also in the envelope was most of the *Dungeon Masters Guide*. Its covers had been torn off, presumably in an act of censorship, and the binding had come loose, but the pages were largely intact. There was something predictably conscientious about the fact that, having dispatched Jun-su to the oblivion of a camp, the authorities had taken pains to return all the relevant documents.

"This is the book that caused all the trouble," said Jun-su.

"Don't start all that again," his mother said impatiently. "You sound like my husband."

Leafing through its pages, Jun-su thought how much his life had been damaged by his chance encounter with this book. It would have been better if he had never seen it. He would have had an unremarkable childhood, with no Teacher Kang, no poetry competitions, no aspirations for fame or praise. He could have worked as a lathe operator, clocking on punctually for his shifts and striving uncomplainingly for the greater glory of the Fatherland. He would have married one of his colleagues and raised a son and a daughter. He could have been a dutiful son and a loyal part of the Kim Il-sung nation. He thought of the families on the beach at Wonsan, making a worthwhile life in spite of everything, or the gatherings during Chuseok, where they honored the generations of ancestors whose forgotten struggles were the real source of their being. Instead, this book had put absurd ideas in his head and made him greedy and ambitious. His life, as a result, had been nothing but vicissitudes and chaos. Everything that might have given it real and lasting meaning had been lost.

Jun-su was about to close the case when he saw an envelope among the old school reports with his name written on it in a familiar hand. For a second, he wondered where he'd seen it before: *frost giant, elemental evil, love potion*. Old Kang's mysterious face loomed out of his memory.

He put it in his pocket.

"Jun-su loves you. He wanted me to tell you that," said Jun-su.

"Of course he does. He's a very good boy," said his mother. "You give him my love."

On the drive home, Jun-su took the envelope from his pocket and opened it. The letter inside was dated April 1997. It had clearly been written after Kang's arrest, while Jun-su was flirting hopelessly with Dr. Park in the sanatorium at the collective farm.

It read:

*I'm guilty of an omission, Jun-su, which I hope to put right with this letter.*

*In the House of Possibility, there is an additional alignment that lies between good and evil.*

*Its adherents regard good and evil as the stuff of fairy tales and propaganda. Few people have the conviction to live in the zone of neutrality. I flatter myself that I am one.*

*I expect by the time you get this, my fate will be decided. I have a good idea which way it will go.*

*I want you to know that I will face my death without fear. I'm a living essence that embraced its destiny.*

*I made my choices. The yut sticks will decide whether I live or die. Win or lose, I know who I am.*

*As for yourself: choose well, Jun-su.*

Su-ok came to see Jun-su again in his apartment at the end of August. The pretext this time was to deliver some papers from the office on behalf of Guk-ju.

"You're spoiling that cat, Jun-su," she said. "She's getting fat."

"She's not fat. She's big-boned," he said. Su-ok had brushed past him lightly on the way in and his arm tingled. Her ineffable scent—flowers, pine bark, ripe peach—made her seem simultaneously desirable and yet impossible to possess. "Does Guk-ju know you're here?" he asked.

"Guk-ju asked me to deliver these," said Su-ok, deliberately misunderstanding his question. "Of course he knows."

"You shouldn't be here alone," said Jun-su. "It looks bad."

"What are you, the *bowibu*?" said Su-ok indignantly.

Jun-su kept thinking about Mr. Shin visiting the apartment to fetch the rule books. How easy it would have been to tape a bug inside one of the portraits, or switch a lightbulb for one with a microphone in it. He imagined Inspector Forearms and

Mr. North wearing headphones, listening to this conversation, scrutinizing it for evidence of disloyalty.

"Have you ever seen an execution?" said Jun-su.

Su-ok frowned. "What are you talking about?" she said.

"If you're lucky," Jun-su went on, "they use nine bullets in your head, back, and knees. If you're not so lucky, they hang you from the end of a rope. And if you're unlucky, the rope is too short to break your neck so you just dangle there for a while shitting yourself, while your face turns black."

Su-ok looked repelled. "Why are you telling me this? Is this because you've met someone else?"

"I'm telling you, comrade," said Jun-su, "because I've conducted self-criticism, and regrettably I understand that my behavior falls short of that required of a party member. From now on, I intend to follow unswervingly the line laid down by our Supreme Leader, Comrade Marshal Kim Jong-un. Thank you for these papers, which you clearly brought in the spirit of single-hearted unity."

He stared at Su-ok with the coldest look he could muster, fighting the urge to take her into his arms. There was no future for them. For her sake, he had to be strong enough to end things.

"Excuse me, comrade. I have to see to my work," he said.

Su-ok covered her mouth with her hand. Tears sprang to her eyes. Her face was distorted with grief and anger. She turned on her heel and left without closing the door.

Jun-su heard her muffled sobs as she passed along the corridor and the sound of other doors opening as residents peered out to see what all the commotion was.

In November, the subject of pets came up at the Daily Life Unity Critique in Jun-su's building.

There was a new superintendent called Mrs. Paek and she seemed determined to impress everyone with her seriousness. Someone had reported seeing Cat's soiled newspaper by the bins. Mrs. Paek had drawn the obvious conclusion.

"First, it's against the rules," she said. "But worse: think what would happen if by some terrible chance the cat dishonored the name of the Supreme Leader, our Comrade Marshal. We'll be collectively responsible. If the illegal cat lover won't come forward, I think we should conduct a search of the building."

The participants looked at each other. No one wanted that to happen: goodness knew what secrets a search might unearth, what contraband goods, South Korean movies and audio files or proscribed literature.

"There's no need to do that," said Jun-su. "The cat's mine. I'm looking after it for a friend. I'll get rid of it."

Later that evening, Jun-su gave Cat a dish of the Russian sprats she liked. Then she sat in his lap while they watched *Take a Look.*

As he stroked her, he put his hand on her throat and felt the purr, turning like a tiny clockwork motor. Jun-su closed his fingers around Cat's thin neck and thought how easily he could end her life.

And suddenly, as if she had read his thoughts, Cat nipped his fingers, making him draw his hand back. She looked reproachfully into his eyes. *Are you out of your mind?* she seemed to be saying. *I'm Cat!*

Jun-su had recently bought a microwave from the hard-currency shop. He still had the box. After the program ended, he put Cat inside it and carried her out of the building.

It had started to snow. Men turned up their collars. Women protected their faces from the cold with gloved hands. Cat was silent, but Jun-su could feel the box's center of gravity change as she moved around inside it.

There was a bus just pulling up to the stop nearest the building. Jun-su got inside. The other passengers looked with poorly concealed envy at this smart young millennial who had the money to buy a Chinese microwave.

Just before the bridge over the Pothong River, Jun-su got off and walked down to the footpath that ran along it. The water closest to the banks was growing thick and syrupy as it froze.

The path curved away along the bank into the darkness. Jun-su had come out impulsively, without putting on gloves or an overcoat, and he could feel the chill through his smart work trousers.

He opened the box and took out Cat. Her fur puffed up to fend off the cold. She felt reassuringly warm in his hands and wriggled, immediately curious to explore. He put her on the ground. Without a look at Jun-su, she began following a scent beside a bush, raising her paws fastidiously over the snow as she went, already scarcely distinguishable from the shadows around her.

Jun-su couldn't bear to watch any longer. He folded the box, turned round, and began walking back. By the time he was climbing the steps of the overpass, he was racked with sobs. He knew he couldn't get on a bus in this condition. Instead he walked in the general direction of the city center. The lights of a distant apartment block twinkled through his frozen eyelashes.

He felt someone take his arm. It was a policeman.

"What is the matter with you, citizen?"

Jun-su wiped his face with his sleeve and tried to compose himself. "I had some bad news in my family, comrade officer," he said.

The officer's severe expression melted into a look of sympathy. "My condolences, citizen," he said, and let him go.

The negotiations over the insurance claim came to a head in mid-December. Guk-ju was sent to London to handle them in person. He asked Jun-su to go with him.

A car arrived at Jun-su's apartment at dawn. At the wheel was the young soldier who had accompanied him on his trips to Changrim. He was wearing a new uniform and he looked excited.

As Jun-su got into the car he went through a mental checklist of everything he needed to bring: his new external passport, his party card, his badge, the memory stick with the paperwork from the office.

The new airport terminal was still under construction, so the driver dropped Jun-su outside the old Soviet-style one.

Guk-ju was already waiting for him in the departure lounge. He was drinking a gin and tonic. "I'm a nervous flyer," he said.

"The Fatherland's pilots are the safest in the world," said Jun-su.

"I think we both know that's not true," said Guk-ju.

Jun-su and Guk-ju were not traveling alone. They were joined by two minders: Mr. Jang, a former national taekwondo champion, and Mr. Oh, who had been trained by the Russian special forces. Mr. Jang and Mr. Oh were booked with Jun-su in economy class, while Guk-ju sat in business class, as befitted his senior status. Jun-su found himself staring at his traveling companions. He was fascinated by Mr. Oh in particular, who had the cold, passionless eyes of someone who had grown used to killing.

Air Choson had been renamed Air Koryo, but the airline was still flying the same old Ilyushin jets, shuttling passengers to Beijing and Vladivostok. In Beijing, the four men transited to an Air China plane.

As they parted on the jetway for the long-haul flight, Guk-ju did something that shocked Jun-su. He unclipped the badge of the Great Leader from his lapel and put it in his pocket. "I suggest you do the same," he said. "It's better to travel incognito."

To Jun-su's surprise, the two minders followed suit.

The flight from Beijing was half-empty, but Mr. Oh and Mr. Jang stuck to their assigned seats next to Jun-su. The three men were in a row together with Jun-su by the window.

Mr. Jang drank wine and whiskey with his meal and then fell asleep watching a Chinese action film. His headphones were half off and his slumbering bulk blocked the row like a broken-down tram. Trapped in his seat, Jun-su lifted up the window blind and watched the wing lights blinking in the darkness. Half an hour before arrival, the plane broke through the clouds into a gray, almost subterranean world. A huge city lay below them, arranged around the serpentine coils of a gleaming river.

The meeting with the insurers took place at an office on the twenty-fifth floor of an enormous silver skyscraper in the heart of the City. It was the holiday season, and the financial district was eerily vacant, like Future Scientist Street late at night. The four men drove in a large minivan with a huge trunk. For this meeting, they proudly wore their badges of the Great Leader.

A towering Christmas tree hung with blinking lights stood in the building's empty lobby. The meeting was scheduled to begin at 9 a.m. Jun-su and Guk-ju made a point of arriving half an hour early, but Mr. Arbuthnot, Mr. Singaratnam, and Mr. Heinz were already waiting for them at a table covered with a selection of pastries. Guk-ju ignored the offering of food and got immediately down to business. The fluency of his English was a shock to Jun-su. So was the way he behaved; it struck Jun-su as very out of character. He was aggressive and contemptuous, questioning the necessity of their trip when everything the insurers had asked for had been supplied to them. Jun-su took a strange pride in Guk-ju's truculence. Here was his boss, a representative of their tiny embattled country, showing the imperialist dogs who was in charge!

The insurers also seemed taken aback by Guk-ju's fierceness. When it was clear that he wouldn't accept any of their principled objections to the payout, they brought up the holiday season. Mr. Singaratnam pleaded that logistical difficulties made the payment impossible. Guk-ju treated this with derision. As a concession, however, he agreed to split the sum into two chunks. "We'll take the first tranche of the money now. I'd call it a goodwill gesture, but things have gone beyond the point where the term seems appropriate," he said with a sneer.

"Our embassy will send someone to collect the balance next week. But we won't be leaving today until we receive the first payment."

Mr. Singaratnam called his colleagues into an adjoining room for a brief consultation. Guk-ju looked pleased with himself and stuffed one of the pastries in his mouth.

They traveled down to the basement in a special lift to collect the money.

According to Jun-su's rough calculations, the ten million euros in one-hundred-euro bills formed a pallet of cash about a meter and a half square and roughly eight hundred kilos in weight. It took Mr. Oh and Mr. Jang more than twenty minutes to load the money into sports bags and bring it out to the waiting car. Guk-ju carried the last bag himself.

Jun-su couldn't take his eyes off the bag as they crossed the courtyard to their vehicle.

"Don't stare at it, brother," said Guk-ju. "You have to act like it's worthless."

The minders followed close behind them. Then they drove in the van to Baker Street.

They pulled in at a luxury hotel, a far cry from the tiny room in the house in Blackheath where Jun-su and the minders were staying.

"Come—this is our moment of triumph," Guk-ju told Jun-su as he hauled one of the bags of cash out of the car. "You must come and enjoy it."

Mr. Oh took the vehicle back to Blackheath, while Mr. Jang traveled up with them in the lift.

The top floor was given over to a single suite. Guk-ju knocked on the door. A young Polish woman answered and let them in.

Inside, sprawled on an enormous purple sofa, was Jimi. He was even more flamboyantly dressed than before, with multiple earrings, a leather jacket, and bandanas tied around both wrists.

Guk-ju lugged the holdall into the room and placed it on the table.

Mr. Jang stood awkwardly at the door.

"Hey, little brother," said Jimi as he caught sight of Jun-su. He summoned Jun-su towards him for a hug. It was a rare honor to be afforded physical intimacy in public with a member of the ruling dynasty. He turned to Guk-ju. "Where's the rest of it?"

"They're paying the balance next week. We have half. The rest of this is going to Geneva in the morning."

Jimi pulled a wad of bills out of the bag. "Almost as good as the Fatherland ones!" he said. Everyone laughed. It was a matter of national pride that the country's forgers were able to produce high-value euro and dollar bills that were indistinguishable from the real thing. "Good work!" Then, turning to Jun-su, he said: "Listen—when do you go back?"

Jun-su glanced at Guk-ju. He wasn't sure what the arrangements were.

"On New Year's Day," said Guk-ju. "The day after tomorrow."

"Perfect, little brother," said Jimi. "Meet me at two p.m. tomorrow. I'm going to show you the city—and I've got a surprise for you."

Mr. Jang and Jun-su slept in the same room at the house belonging to the Korean National Insurance Corporation in Blackheath. It was normal for the country's representatives to live communally when they went abroad. But Jun-su was under a more than ordinary degree of supervision. It was obvious that Mr. Jang had instructions not to let Jun-su out of his sight. Mr. Jang only relaxed his guard once they were back in the house. There was no way to leave the building without being observed. A large metal gate stood at the end of the driveway, and two men took turns at sentry duty inside the entrance hall.

At midmorning the next day, Mr. Jang and Jun-su drove into the city. They were much too early, but the idea of keeping a member of the royal family waiting was simply unthinkable. Now, with two hours to spare, Jun-su persuaded Mr. Jang to come with him to a museum. The request made Mr. Jang suspicious and he stuck closely to Jun-su as he wandered through the empty rooms of the National Portrait Gallery.

The woman at the ticket desk told Jun-su that entry was

free, but she reminded him that they would be closing early as it was New Year's Eve.

Jun-su wasn't sure why he'd suggested the gallery. But he knew that if he'd left it up to Mr. Jang, they would have sat in a café for two hours, each nursing a single coffee, while they waited for Jimi to show up.

Mr. Jang yawned loudly. The wood floors creaked as he shuffled through the rooms.

Jun-su stopped in front of a portrait. It was a picture of a government official from the days of Tudor England. The courtier had a guarded, watchful face that reminded Jun-su of his colleagues in Office 39. A plaque beside the painting informed him that the sitter had been beheaded for treason in 1535.

By the time they reached Wunjo Guitars on Denmark Street, Jimi was already there. Mr. Jang looked flustered about this, but Jimi didn't care in the slightest. He was sitting on an amplifier, running through some licks on a white guitar.

Mr. Jang and Jun-su sat down and watched Jimi try a range of different instruments.

The sales assistant, a tall, skinny man in a plaid shirt, was clearly impressed with his skills. "Nice," he said approvingly. "Slowhand."

"That's right. We're going to see him tonight. I'm taking my little brother." Jimi nodded in Jun-su's direction. Jimi had altered his accent slightly and was speaking with a mannered mid-Atlantic drawl.

"Seriously? I didn't know he was playing. Is he at the Hootenanny?"

"No. Special invitation-only event," said Jimi with a trace of smugness.

"Oh—that charity thing."

"Yes," said Jimi. "Rumor is that it's the last one."

Jun-su stood up to stretch his legs. He'd been sitting for about fifteen minutes. Mr. Jang immediately jumped up too.

Jimi laughed. "Calm down!" he said in Korean to the minder. "Little brother is not running anywhere! Even if he gets out of the door—where will he go?"

It was true. Beyond the threshold was a land of infinite strangeness, a world of possibilities that Jun-su had been taught to fear since childhood. He had a feeling that entering its atmosphere unprotected might even be fatal to him, as though he were an astronaut removing his helmet in space. His head would swell up and his brains would begin to bubble out of his ears.

"I'll take this one," said Jimi, indicating one of the guitars.

"The Nocaster," said the assistant. "A collector's item. Excellent choice."

* * *

Slowhand was the nickname of Jimi's favorite living guitarist, an Englishman named Eric Clapton. During an early dinner at a Japanese restaurant, Jimi told Jun-su something of his history. He was as passionate on this subject as Jun-su had ever seen him.

"Only person to be in the Rock and Roll Hall of Fame three times. He is my god. No one can call *him* an NPC." Jimi chuckled and gave Jun-su a knowing look. It was clear that Hans's insult had not been forgotten.

Jimi explained that Slowhand had had drinking problems that affected his health. As a reward to the people who had helped him give up alcohol, he played a concert every New Year's Eve at an auditorium in the south of the city. It was a very intimate occasion and it had taken the country's diplomats a long time to wangle tickets. Alcohol was strictly banned from the venue.

"Which means one thing," said Jimi.

"No drinking?" suggested Jun-su.

"No, little brother. It means get drunk now!"

In addition to all the sake they drank with their meal, Jimi opened a bottle of cognac in the car which they passed between them on the drive to Woking.

Mr. Jang didn't drink at all. He sat in the front seat next to the driver, a man with the sturdy build of a *bowibu* who was based in London at the embassy in Ealing. Now and again, Jun-su was aware of the driver glancing at him in the rearview mirror.

They arrived in the car park of the Woking Leisure Centre around 8 p.m. The driver asked them to wait in the car, while he carried out a final security check on the venue. Mr. Jang got out with him.

Jimi took another swig of cognac and passed the bottle to Jun-su. It was still about two-thirds full. Jun-su gripped the neck, read the label, and sloshed the liquid around inside. In his hand, the thick bottle suddenly had the heft of a weapon. For a terrible instant, he imagined what it would be like to smash the bottle into Jimi's handsome face. Through the steamed-up windows, Jun-su could see Mr. Jang's back as he stood guard outside the vehicle.

"Long life, little brother," said Jimi.

Jun-su swigged the cognac. He offered the bottle back to Jimi, who shook his head. It occurred to Jun-su that Jimi's drinking didn't have quite the reckless, self-annihilating quality that it sometimes did. He was energized by the prospect of being close to his hero.

"We're like spies for the Fatherland," said Jun-su. "We're in enemy territory on an important mission." But he was thinking that, through the misted glass, the people in coats arriving for the concert were indistinguishable from a crowd in Pyongyang. "What an adventure," Jun-su added. "Thank you."

Jimi clapped him on the shoulder and looked him in the eyes. Then he took back the bottle and turned it over in his hands. He was silent for a while. "I know about you and Su-ok," he said finally.

"Me and Su-ok?" said Jun-su.

"Don't play with me, little brother. She confessed to everything. Eventually."

Jun-su lowered his eyes and began rubbing at a spot of cognac on the upholstery. He tried to make his face still and masklike.

"It was never going to happen between me and her," said Jimi. "That's why she did it. I understand. She needs a companion who can give her what she needs. It's like Eric and Pattie Boyd. There's passion, but it's not practical. My family never approved anyway. They've told me to clean up my act. I'm going to be helping my brother out more and taking a bigger role in the department from now on. There are going to be more trips like this one."

Jun-su watched a young couple walking arm-in-arm through the car park, heedless of their proximity to a prince of the Mount Paektu lineage. Jimi put the cognac bottle down on the seat between them.

"We'll be relying on you as well. Guk-ju tells me you've done great work for my family. So I want to reward you in my way too. I want you to have Su-ok."

Jun-su scrutinized Jimi's face, trying not to reveal his own feelings. What did Jimi mean by this? He couldn't help dwelling on the ominous sentence about Su-ok. *She confessed to everything. Eventually.*

"I'm saying you can have Su-ok," said Jimi. "As long as you understand that I have to satisfy my needs as a man with her." He paused to let the magnanimity of his offer sink in. "What do you say to that?"

"How does Su-ok feel about it?" said Jun-su.

"I think it's what she wants. I think she really loves you, little brother. But there are things that only I can give her. And she understands that this is how things have to be."

Every year that Slowhand played the Woking Leisure Centre, he booked the venue under the name of a different made-up band. That night it was "Happy Destiny."

Jun-su couldn't make sense of his feelings as he followed Mr. Jang into the building. It certainly didn't feel like he was arriving at a happy destiny. But at least, if Su-ok could consent to something, it meant that she was alive and unhurt. That was some consolation.

Slowhand began the concert by duetting with a woman he introduced as his aunt, Sylvia Clapp. The song was called "I'll Walk Beside You." The audience whistled appreciatively as they started. Slowhand played about a dozen songs, and then announced an intermission.

Jimi had slipped out of the auditorium a few minutes before the interval. Now he returned. From the way he was sniffing and rubbing his nose, Jun-su deduced that he'd gone to the car to get high.

"The jet lag is really catching up with me," said Jun-su. "I could use something to wake me up."

Jimi took the hint. He reached into the pocket of his leather jacket, but his hand lingered. "Promise me you won't go crazy, little brother," he said.

"I just want to get into the spirit," said Jun-su.

Jimi punched his shoulder lightly. "I'm kidding, little brother! I'm glad you're cutting loose for once." He passed Jun-su a small, flat metal case that was designed for carrying business cards.

"Coming?" said Jun-su.

Jimi shook his head. "Just be careful. We don't want to get kicked out."

Jun-su nodded. Mr. Jang followed him into the men's room at a respectful distance and waited while Jun-su went into one of the cubicles.

*It's what she wants. And she understands that this is how it has to be.*

Jun-su laid the metal case on the cistern. The frosted window behind it was almost black. The sky beyond was covered with a lid of cloud, but above that, he knew, hung points of starlight.

*In the darkness before the yut sticks do their work*, Jun-su thought, *we are nothing: neither Cat, nor fox, nor Yankee bastard, nor troll, nor pure-blooded descendant of Tangun.* In the moment before you first drew breath, you were only a quickening pulse, one point in an unthinkable vastness of stars. Who decided how it had to be? Who chose your destiny?

An old memory surfaced from the depths of his brain: Teacher Kang, pouring yut sticks from hand to hand and tutting as he did so. "Really," the old man was saying, "is this any time to be practical?"

Jun-su lowered the seat of the toilet and stepped up quietly onto the ledge behind.

The drop from the window was higher than he expected. Jun-su slipped as he landed and tore a hole in the knee of his trousers. He immediately got to his feet and started to run. It had been rainy and blustery for most of the day. The wet grass underfoot soaked his Chinese-made dress shoes. Away to his left, he could see the lights of the car park. He recalled that an exit road curved south from there and led, somehow, back to the city.

Mr. Jang would grow suspicious when Jun-su failed to emerge, but the toilets were crowded with other concertgoers. The spectacle of an Asian man in a suit smashing his shoulder against a cubicle door would attract unwanted attention.

How long would Mr. Jang wait? Five minutes? Ten minutes? Would he bide his time until Slowhand resumed the second set and the toilets emptied completely? Whenever he finally managed to open the door, he would find his boss's drug stash untouched on the cistern and the window above it raised to make a Jun-su-sized aperture. Jun-su could so easily imagine the disbelief on Jimi's face as Mr. Jang broke the news of his betrayal. They would certainly go after him, and there would be no reprieve for him this time if they caught him.

While Jun-su was tempted to stick to the road they had arrived by, he understood it would leave him very exposed. Anyone pursuing him in a car would quickly cancel out his head start, so Jun-su turned his back on the car park, scaled a low fence, and ran towards the line of trees that lay just to the north.

Rain was falling thickly now. Gusts of wind rattled and shook the bare branches of the oaks and plane trees. The curious English damp penetrated his thin suit jacket: he'd left his overcoat in the car. His grazed knee throbbed. Beneath his feet, the ground seemed to move very swiftly. Just beyond the trees lay a footpath. Jun-su instinctively followed it west. It curved through the woodland for about half a kilometer before it met a narrow road, hemmed in by tall hedgerows.

Jun-su stepped out onto the road. The soles of his shoes clicked on the wet tarmac as he broke into a jog. Hearing the sound of an engine approaching, he turned his face towards the bushes to hide it. The car passed him noisily and disappeared, its high beams illuminating the road ahead of it with a wall of light. Jun-su's hands were shaking. The adrenaline had sobered him completely. The next vehicle would surely bring Mr. Jang and the driver from the embassy. Finding him alone on a road in darkness, they would punish him without mercy.

Hair plastered to his scalp, Jun-su continued along the slippery road, struggling to keep his footing. His lungs burned. Around him the leafless trees bent in the wind. Beyond them, as if mocking his loneliness, stood handsome suburban dwellings, adorned with festive lights.

At a fork in the road, a signpost said: WHITE ROSE LANE. In Jun-su's mind, the petals of a white flower unfurled in the hot water of a teacup. "Your bosom is a bosom that blooms," said a voice, "and embroiders our leader's great will into the earth!" He saw the face of the Dear Leader. "You honored me with a poem about my birthplace. It is enough." The Dear Leader was exhausted. His face was caked in makeup, but it couldn't conceal his tiredness. He gazed at Jun-su with a look of infinite grief. Now the road began sloping uphill. White Rose Lane opened onto a junction with a parade of shops, where a gaggle of revelers draped in tinsel and carrying bottles lurched past on high heels. They were all headed the same way. Jun-su fell in step with them as they walked onto the brightly lit platform of Woking Station. Together they boarded a packed train, fuggy with the warmth of bodies, damp coats, and the alcoholic fumes of inebriated passengers.

Jun-su looked nervously about. Who among the passengers might be North Korean spies? At New Malden, three Asian passengers got on: two men in their thirties and a younger woman with bobbed hair. *She confessed to everything. Eventually.* A memory flashed through Jun-su's mind of his time in camp: another execution, and the prisoners compelled by the guards to disfigure the dead man's body by flinging stones.

Wiping the condensation from the window, he gazed out into the darkness beyond. The train snaked through the suburbs of southwest London, rattling past the backs of houses, through cuttings overgrown with ivy and elder, as the buildings grew taller and grander and they approached the heart of the city.

At Waterloo Station, the train disgorged its passengers and Jun-su followed them through the unmanned barriers. The concourse was as bright as daylight and teeming with people.

Crowds were assembling to greet the New Year. There was something extraordinary in the atmosphere: a recklessness bordering on chaos, a crazed, bacchanalian energy.

Jun-su looked up at one of the CCTV cameras that covered every inch of the station. He knew the intelligence agents of his country were terrifyingly resourceful. They had managed to abduct dozens of Japanese citizens from the beaches of their native country, spiriting them away in boats. A few years later, the half-brother of the Supreme Leader would be murdered openly with poison in a Malaysian airport. They shared intelligence with the Chinese, and were capable of hacking into spy satellites. The security cameras of a British railway station would present little challenge.

He was certain that several dozen agents had been sent to London to guard Jimi during his visit. It had been at least an hour since Jun-su had fled. The alarm had undoubtedly been raised by now. Nothing about the likely direction of Jun-su's escape was hard to guess. Every potential defector had a standing offer of sanctuary at the South Korean Embassy and was certain to head there by the quickest route possible. By now, agents would certainly be in place outside it.

At one of the station's exits, Jun-su studied a map, trying to make sense of the haphazard loops of the city.

"You lost, mate?" said a booming voice behind him. It belonged to a tall man in a leopard-print suit and a bowler hat. Jun-su was enveloped by waves of his cologne. The man's cheeks gleamed pinkly above his carefully tended beard and mustache. Jun-su felt suddenly self-conscious about his own damp and bedraggled appearance. Beside the man in the leopard print stood a man dressed as a Roman legionary, complete with plastic sword and crested helmet; he was talking loudly into a mobile phone. "Where are you trying to get to?" said the leopard-print man.

"Shad Thames," said Jun-su, enunciating the words carefully.

"Shad Thames," echoed the man, and clapped his hand over his forehead. "Oh, I know that. Darren: Shad Thames?"

The Roman legionary lowered his phone for a second. "It's near the Horny Man," Jun-su heard him say.

"What, *Dulwich*?" Leopard-print man sounded outraged.

"No. The other one. Butler's Wharf."

As the two men argued over the best route, Jun-su looked anxiously across the concourse: an Asian man in a dark suit was walking purposefully through the crowd, scanning the faces around him. Everything about his demeanor confirmed Jun-su's instinct: *bowibu*.

Jun-su immediately took to his heels, fleeing from the station through the press of people gathering for the fireworks. A few voices protested as he tried to burrow through the drunk, carefree bodies that were blocking his progress. He kept glancing behind him for any sign of his pursuers.

After a few minutes running, he altered his route abruptly, ducking away from the crowds and into the backstreets that ran parallel to the river. Wherever he went, he couldn't shake the ominous sense of being hunted. The shadows seemed alive with concealed *bowibu* agents.

At midnight, the first fireworks fizzed into the sky over the river and burst into yellow and red flowers. Jun-su flinched as he heard the sound of the bangs. Light unfolded over the sky, and the smoke that drifted over the crowds smelt to Jun-su like the aftermath of an execution.

As he followed Montague Close around Southwark Cathedral towards London Bridge, he heard purposeful steps behind him. A dull blow landed between his shoulder blades. He fell forward. The damp cobbles grazed his face. He curled himself into a ball.

"Traitor dog," grunted a gruff voice. Something sharp stabbed him in the kidneys and emitted an electric shock. The pain seemed to light him up from the inside. A knee pinned him to the ground while a pair of strong hands folded his left arm into an agonizing knot.

"Help!" Jun-su shouted feebly. "Help!"

There were two of them. They lifted him to his feet.

A handful of passersby, disturbed by the commotion, moved hesitantly towards them. A woman was the first to speak. "What are you doing?" she asked the men.

"This man thief. This man steal," said one of Jun-su's captors. "Bad this man." In the force of his words was the justified rage of the affronted patriot, the true believer's hatred of the apostate.

"Who are you?" asked the woman, emboldened by the rising indignation of the crowd that had begun to gather. She pointed at one of the *bowibu*.

Jun-su struggled to speak. He pleaded with the crowd: "I don't know this man. Please, help me."

"Get off him, bruv," said a voice. Mobile phones were raised to record the incident. The man holding Jun-su let him go to push one away.

"We are police," said one of the agents, but now there was a note of anxiety in his voice.

"Show us your warrant card."

"This man terrorist!" said the other agent. Together they tried to maneuver Jun-su away from the crowd.

Now hands intervened to separate Jun-su from his captors. He felt his jacket tear as the crowd pulled him away.

"Is this yours, fam?" A woman was holding out Jun-su's phone. It had fallen from his pocket in the scuffle.

Jun-su grimaced. The phone. How could he have been so stupid? He'd been carrying it since he'd fled the concert, unwittingly emitting an electronic scent that they had been using to track his movements. "It belongs to them," he said. And he sprinted away into the darkness.

The flat Jun-su was looking for was in a converted warehouse called Galingale Place. It stood right on the river. Once it had been used to store chests of imported spices after their arrival at the docks. Old iron lifting equipment still protruded from its brickwork, but now it housed the kind of luxury flats that were favored by London's own *donju*, the masters of money who worked just across the river in the financial district.

Jun-su went up in a lift. At the end of a corridor, music thumped from behind a half-open door. He pushed it open and was met by a wave of warm air, scented with perfume and alcohol. The apartment was full of people dancing.

At the far side of the packed living room, a dark-skinned man in his thirties was standing behind a pair of turntables. He bobbed his head in time to the music as he raised the volume of one of his faders.

Weaving between the dancers, Jun-su crossed the room until he was standing in front of the sound system. The dark-skinned man glanced up at him, puzzled by the arrival of this breathless and rain-sodden apparition in a suit.

"Hello," said Jun-su.

"Sorry, mate, I'm a bit mashed," said the man, removing his headphones. "Who are you?"

"My name is Cho Jun-su," said Jun-su.

The man leaned forward to hear better.

Jun-su repeated himself.

The man shook his head. "You sure you're in the right place, Chojun?"

"I think so," said Jun-su, still breathing heavily. "I believe that in 1991 you visited Wonsan and stayed at the Songdowon Hotel."

The man stepped away from the turntables and laid an arm on Jun-su's shoulders. The weight of it carried an implicit threat. "Mate, I think you might be at the wrong party."

Jun-su reached into his breast pocket and took out an envelope. From it, he removed a single sheet of paper.

It was the crumpled title page of the *Dungeon Masters Guide*. Torn carefully from the book, and creased from repeated folding, it still bore the name of its former owner: Fidel Olatunji-Kapsberger, in both a grandiose cursive and a laboriously conceived array of Elvish runes.

For a very long time, Fidel looked in disbelief at the fragment, until he finally raised his eyes and turned his astonished gaze on Cho Jun-su.

# HAPPY DESTINY

It was David and Chibundo Kapsberger's habit to welcome the New Year with a small gathering of old friends at their handsome townhouse in Islington.

By the time Fidel and Jun-su arrived, it was nearly 2 a.m. Most of the guests had left and the atmosphere had grown a little sour. David and a bespectacled man with a white beard were having a furious argument over some detail of political arcana while Chibundo pointedly cleared up around them. She was collecting champagne bottles and putting them noisily into recycling bags in the hope that the final guest, an academic called Lionel Figes, would take the hint. She brightened up at the arrival of her son, welcoming him on the doorstep with a hearty embrace.

Watching mother and son hug, Jun-su felt a pang. It was painful to think about his own mother, eating a cheerless New

Year's lunch in the hospital in Changrim. And not for the first or last time, he questioned the sense of what he was doing.

"Your father and Lionel are going at it in the front room," said Chibundo wearily.

"I think I've got something that'll distract them," said Fidel. "Mum, this is Jun-su."

"Happy New Year, Jun-su," said Chibundo, as if he were a frequent and honored guest.

Jun-su followed Fidel down the hallway into the overpowering warmth of the drawing room. A coal fire was glowing in the hearth. Jun-su inhaled the scent of pine needles and mulled wine. A large fir tree, draped with baubles, lights, and tangles of glittery ribbon, stood by the bay window.

"—which is my point in the book!" David was saying, as he refilled his glass generously from the wine bottle. His teeth had turned gray from the tannins in the red wine. "True socialism has never been tried."

"Except for all the times that it has," said Lionel, gesturing so violently with his glass that a little whiskey splashed onto the rug. "When are you going to be honest enough to admit that Marx got it wrong? Life isn't some march towards a glorious future utopia. It's a tragic business that involves impossible choices—"

"—says the reactionary defeatist. Where would we be if we all had that attitude? I tell you where: my wife would be a second-class citizen in this country and children would be dying inside chimneys. Sometimes I despair of you, Lionel." David slurped his wine, and noticed Fidel. Jun-su was taken aback by the lack of warmth in his eyes. "Ah, speaking of the exploiter class, here's my son, the hedge fund manager. To what do we owe this rare pleasure?"

"I came to get your advice," said Fidel.

Lionel looked from father to son warily and stood up, clearly taking Fidel's arrival as his cue to leave. Fidel raised a hand to stop him.

"Actually, you might be able to help as well," said Fidel. "This is Jun-su. He's seeking political asylum."

"Political asylum?" said David in a tone of incredulity. "Where from?"

"North Korea," said Jun-su.

"Why?" asked David.

"Dad, what's wrong with you? You've been there. I've been there. You know what it's like. Weren't you an asylum seeker once?"

"Touché," burbled Lionel happily into his whiskey.

"That was a bit different. I had an ideological disagreement with the US government over the prosecution of an illegal war that I wanted no part of."

Lionel cocked his hand over his ear theatrically as though he'd heard the sound of a gunshot in the street. "There it is! The authentic note of left-wing sanctimony, capable of shedding tears over some abstract figures in a camp in Calais, but reluctant to lift a finger when an actual refugee from a totalitarian dictatorship turns up on his doorstep."

"I didn't say I *wouldn't* help," said David. "Jun-su—would you mind stepping outside for a moment?"

Standing in the hall, Jun-su admired the sisal runner on the painted stairs, the framed Soviet propaganda posters, and the Nigerian barbershop signs on the walls. The discussion was taking a long time. Jun-su pressed his ear against the door.

"He *says* he's an asylum seeker," David was saying. "Just think about what you're getting yourself into. We don't know anything about his real circumstances."

"Look, I know what I'm going to do," said Fidel. "This isn't a hard decision for me. I just thought you might have a contact at the South Korean Embassy."

"I think you're being naïve."

"I think you're being a dick."

Jun-su heard creaking from the stairs and moved away from the door. Chibundo Kapsberger stood above him on the landing. "I'm going to bed, dear," she said.

"Good night," said Jun-su.

At that moment, the door to the living room opened. Fidel emerged, shaking his head. "It's sorted. Lionel's got a number for someone at the embassy."

That night, Jun-su slept fitfully in Fidel's old bedroom. It was at the top of the house, with just enough room for a single bed, a desk, a cupboard, and shelves crowded with old textbooks on finance and business management. On a distant upper shelf, too high for regular dusting, stood an array of painted metal figures. Jun-su took one down. It was heavy in his palm, a barbarian fighter, naked except for boots and a loincloth like a sumo wrestler's. The figure held a two-handed broadsword cocked over his right shoulder.

*Why?* David Kapsberger had asked. *How?* was the better question. How did someone created by one reality begin to operate by the rules of another? Every connection that had given Jun-su's life meaning was about to be severed. He thought of Cat, her high fastidious steps making dints in the snow as she moved away from him without a backwards glance.

"I replaced the book when I got home," Fidel was saying as he sipped coffee from a paper cup. "But it was a kind of secret vice with me. For some reason, it always seemed to be a choice between role-playing games and girls. Plus Dad didn't approve."

"I really don't appreciate being portrayed as some totalitarian Mr. Nyet," said David from the back seat. "It's a totally false characterization."

"You said it was a waste of time."

"That doesn't even sound like something I'd say."

"Whatever," said Fidel.

Fidel drove a Mercedes like the ones popular among high-ranking party functionaries back in North Korea. He had picked up Jun-su from the house in Islington a few minutes after eleven o'clock. The four of them, Jun-su, David, Fidel, and Lionel, were now sitting in it, waiting for a call from Lionel's contact at the embassy. Everyone apart from Jun-su was scratchy from lack of sleep. Jun-su was simply frightened.

They were parked by a row of townhouses on Petty France, a few hundred meters from the South Korean Embassy.

Lionel's phone rang. "He's there," he said. "He says it's important that you go on your own, but he'll be waiting for you. It'll be very smooth."

Jun-su exhaled nervously. "I'm worried about *bowibu*."

"Do you really think they'd bother?" said David.

"Shut up, Dad," Fidel said. He looked at Jun-su. "This is a free country. They can't do anything to you. You'll be fine."

Jun-su stepped out of the car and closed the door behind him. He was wearing the same clothes he'd had on the previous morning, when he'd left Blackheath for the rendezvous with Jimi. Both Kapsbergers had offered him clothes, but they were taller and more heavily built than he was. He shivered as he made his way down the empty pavement. The weather had brightened up after the previous day's rain but the temperature had dropped to close to freezing. Cold air blew through the hole in the knee of his trousers.

His contact, Mr. Min, was supposed to meet him by the

back exit and bring him inside. There was no sign of anyone. The foyer of the embassy was empty and the windows were dark. Suddenly he was aware of a voice shouting in Korean.

"I thought I'd find you here." It was Jimi. He was standing beside a large SUV. Dark glasses concealed his eyes, but his blotchy skin and hoarse voice betrayed a sleepless night. "What are you doing, little brother? You can't be serious about this."

Jun-su looked around. He was out of sight and earshot of his allies.

"Get in the car and we can discuss this," said Jimi.

"Nothing to discuss, brother. My mind's made up."

"*Brother*. How can you use that word? When you say it, I feel disgusted. What kind of brother does this? You're spitting on your own face. You know how defectors live? No family. No friends. Their lives have no meaning at all. You become nothing."

"That's what I've chosen. To be nothing."

Jimi looked puzzled. "I see the reports. You know how many defectors beg to be allowed to come home? I could live here if I wanted. I know this world, I belong here more than you, and I choose to live where I do."

"I'm not you," said Jun-su.

"What about Su-ok?"

"That's up to her. I know how much she loves you. She talks about nothing else."

In spite of himself, Jimi seemed to soften.

At that moment, the side door of the embassy opened. A middle-aged man gestured apologetically at Jun-su and beckoned him inside.

"And your father and mother?" shouted Jimi. "What kind of son are you? I can make this okay for you if you leave with me now, but once you go in there, it's over. Don't spit on your own face, Jun-su!"

Rage disfigured Jimi's handsome features. The tall buildings faded into darkness. Their windows became gold gleams shining by torchlight in cavern walls. Jun-su looked around him. To his left lay the body of Gumiho the Bold, bleeding out from an axe wound to the throat.

*Serve me and live!* a voice seemed to say. An involuntary smile formed on Jun-su's lips.

"Don't laugh at me, human scum," yelled Jimi. "You're worse than a dog, and I'll make sure you die like one."

Jun-su entered the embassy. The door closed behind him and silenced the stream of threats. The last words he remembered hearing were: "You'll regret this forever, Jun-su."

By a quirk of history, the suburb of New Malden in southwest London is home to a small Korean diaspora from both the South and the North.

There are more North Korean asylum seekers here than anywhere else in the world outside Seoul. At least, that's the claim.

For a number of geopolitical and personal reasons, I found myself one spring, not long ago, unable to do my job. Not wanting to sit around at home, I registered online to do voluntary work for the National Health Service. I was selected to deliver groceries to the housebound, vulnerable, and largely Korean-speaking older residents of the neighborhood.

This is how I ended up making the acquaintance of a man called Joseph Cho.

Joseph was a pharmacist. I would pick up prescriptions from him at the chemist's on Merton High Street and deliver them to people who were stuck at home.

One morning as I waited behind the Plexiglas screen for Joseph to fill an order, I asked him where exactly he'd grown up.

"Not far from Seoul," he said. I learned later that this was a white lie he often told on meeting someone for the first time.

I explained to him that I'd visited South Korea in my work as a filmmaker. A few years earlier, I'd made a program about the Sinan archipelago that lies west of the port city of Mokpo. It's a place where people with mental disabilities had been trafficked as slaves to work on the islands' salt farms.

"This happens in Korea?" he said, with real surprise in his voice.

I felt a bit bad for bringing up such an unpleasant aspect of his native country. I wanted to reassure him that in spite of the darkness of that story, I'd come back with a positive impression. I told him what a good time I'd had, how well we'd eaten, how impressed I was with the country, and how eager I was to go back one day to Hanguk—the Korean word for Korea.

Joseph smiled, but not, as I suspected, because of my terrible pronunciation. "I'm not from Hanguk," he said. "I'm from Choson." And he looked at me to see how I would react.

I felt an extraordinary sense of excitement. I knew that Choson was the word for their country used by the people of the North. "Oh my goodness," I said. "You're from the strangest place on earth." I tried not to be too voracious in my curiosity, but it was hard to conceal my amazement.

The next time I came, I brought a copy of one of my novels that had been translated into Korean. The gift of the book broke the ice between us. Joseph was fascinated by the story, which takes place in northern Siberia, and read it gratifyingly quickly. He was curious about the act of imagination behind it. I explained that it was partly based on landscapes I'd seen, but that most of it was simply made up.

"You studied writing at university?" asked Joseph, as he folded over the tops of the paper bags containing the prescribed medicines and lined them up in a big cardboard tray for me to take out to my car.

"No. If anything, I learned how to write from playing Dungeons & Dragons with my friends," I said.

The crackling of the paper bags stopped abruptly. Joseph looked at me with curiosity.

"It's quite hard to explain," I warned him. "I'll try to give you the short version: it's basically a game of make-believe that you play with special dice."

"I know what it is," Joseph said. And then he added: "Believe it or not, I used to play that game."

That's how I learned about Joseph's previous life as Cho Jun-su and the extraordinary encounter with the game that had shaped his destiny. Over the subsequent week or so, I began arriving earlier and earlier so I could hear more installments of his tale. During my deliveries, I would turn the story over and over in my head, marveling at it.

There were, however, aspects of Joseph's life that he was reluctant to talk about. Prison in particular. It seemed to me that this had been the watershed experience from which he had emerged transformed, but he seemed loath to discuss it.

One of the few times he raised the subject was when I asked him if he knew what had become of his old nemesis, Seo Tae-il.

It turned out that five years into his sentence, Jun-su had got a relatively cushy part-time job in the prison administration building.

The prison guards were chosen above all for their political loyalty and physical strength; they tended to lack the patience for paperwork. Word had got around that Jun-su was an educated man. As a favor to a guard, he completed the accounts for the prison rabbit farm, its distillery, and the autumn collection of wild ginseng that was sold to generate revenue.

Jun-su did the work so well that when an order came in to reorganize the camp's filing systems and transfer the information to newfangled Chinese computers, he was selected to help. It meant two days a week indoors for several months over the summer and, if Jun-su could string out the assignment, possibly more. His hope was that he could find a way to keep it going through the winter and into the difficult spring. Spring was in some ways the hardest time of all. At that point in the year, the food reserves would all have been used up and nothing edible would have yet sprouted. Finding a place to stay warm for a few hours a day was the kind of thing that, in the harsh, existential bookkeeping of camp—calories in, calories expended—made the difference between life and death.

Better still, Jun-su was usually left entirely on his own in the tiny office: there was no soap in the camp and the guards naturally avoided being in confined spaces with their malodorous charges. Sometimes there was even discarded food in the wastebasket: fruit peelings, bones, scraps of dried fish.

One hot summer day, typing up the long intake lists, Jun-su found himself staring at the name Seo Tae-il.

It's not an unusual Korean name, but the place of birth—Wonsan—and the date—six months earlier than Jun-su's—confirmed his hunch that it was the Tae-il of his childhood.

The discovery stirred up a riot of feelings: glee at the poetic justice it entailed; curiosity at what had caused the fall from grace; and then, in spite of everything, a pulse of reluctant sympathy. Tae-il had ended up in the Zone of Total Control, the hell of the irredeemables, from which no release was possible.

Jun-su approached the guard who was overseeing his assignment and explained that a number of the carbon copies he was working from were illegible. Was it possible for someone to go and check his lists against the originals?

"Go yourself," was the surly reply. It was all the permission that Jun-su needed.

He set out early the next day, walking into the neighboring valley and arriving there around lunchtime. "I have orders to report to the administration building," he told a guard.

Jun-su's purplish jacket marked him out as a visitor, but he was still troubled by a misgiving that he would somehow be unable to return to his own zone. At the administration building, he explained that he was confirming some records. He'd brought a selection, of which Seo Tae-il's was one. When the administrator inevitably confirmed the accuracy of his information, Jun-su said: "I need to speak to him in person."

The administrator didn't question the necessity of this. He directed him to the appropriate building.

In the Zone of Total Control, all pretence at rehabilitation had been dropped. The prisoners were spared political education. There were not even any portraits of the Great and Dear Leaders.

The absence of any hope was intended to crush the spirits

of the prisoners, whose life expectancies were very short. However, it also had the effect of making them reckless. The guards were armed with rifles instead of pistols and watched their charges with much greater vigilance.

Eventually Jun-su found his way to the correct dormitory. Its overlord was a trusted prisoner who, in return for meager privileges, was expected to keep an eye on his fellow inmates. Jun-su explained that he wanted to speak to Seo Tae-il. "What do you need with that scumbag?" said the prisoner as he sorted through a handful of cigarette butts.

"Administrative business," said Jun-su.

"He's the worst of them all," said the prisoner. "You'll find him in there." With a nod of his head, he indicated a wooden box standing apart from the residential buildings.

Jun-su's immediate thought was that it was a latrine, and that Seo Tae-il was either using it or cleaning it.

In fact, neither assumption was correct. It was an instrument of torture, and Seo Tae-il was being punished.

Jun-su could hear murmuring as he approached the box. It was the sound of dehydrated lips muttering some kind of incantation. Clearly, Seo Tae-il had lost his mind.

"Tae-il?" shouted Jun-su. "Are you in there?"

The sound stopped. For four or five seconds, there was silence. Then the crazy droning resumed.

Jun-su banged on the side of the hut with his balled fist. "It's me. Cho Jun-su."

This time the sound stopped for a long time. Finally a husky voice spoke. "Cho Jun-su?"

Jun-su peered through the chinks of the wood. The heat inside was terrible. Tae-il's eyes were yellow with jaundice and his big frame seemed to be nothing but hide and sticks.

The awful eyes lit on Jun-su. "Praise God. I prayed for this moment. Forgive me, Cho Jun-su. Will you pray with me?"

"Will I what?"

"Pray with me, Jun-su." Tae-il closed his eyes and began muttering again, the same mysterious incantation as before.

Jun-su had been brought up to regard religious practice as an abomination, but he silently acquiesced, standing there until the prayer was concluded and the yellow, bloodshot eyes had once again opened. Even in the terrible dehydration of the sweatbox, Tae-il's eyes moistened and he once more asked to be forgiven.

In Joseph's telling, this was indeed the formative moment of his prison experience. By the time I met him, he was a committed Christian and a regular congregant at the Calvary Korean Church in New Malden.

I was surprised by my own reaction to the revelation: I found it slightly disappointing. To me, it diminished Joseph's resourcefulness to give any of the credit for his survival to a divinity.

Joseph found my awkwardness around the subject of religion perplexing. He took my unbelief as a challenge and was keen to evangelize me. "Jesus is a good guy, Marcel. We need to talk about this."

In a way that I hoped was friendly rather than contemptuous, I fended off his efforts and tried to explain that growing up in a kind of cult had perhaps left him with a need for an overarching story that made sense of everything.

"Maybe," he said. "The way I understand it, the message of Jesus is simple: no NPCs."

I had to confess I was attracted by the originality of this interpretation. I told him that his Christianity evidently owed as much to Gary Gygax as to the four evangelists.

He enjoyed that. "I've thought that many times," he said. "In fact, the essence of my faith is that none of us is truly real. We are not real, but what we do to each other *is* real."

I couldn't hide my look of bafflement.

"It's a paradox," he said. "And though I believe it's true, I don't fully understand it myself. All I know for sure is that the fundamental sin is to treat someone as if they are not real."

"Even though they aren't?" I asked, trying not to sound perplexed.

"Exactly!" he said. "So you see, this was the real crime of my country. To treat its people as NPCs. Someone can choose to serve—this is a beautiful thing. But being *made* to serve—this is slavery. I've told you that my country was always full of people waiting, people waiting for transport, for rations, for on-the-spot guidance. But Jesus already came! Our job is not to wait, it is to be a good person. This is the struggle everywhere. The task is somehow to become real."

"How?"

"Now you are asking an interesting question. Only by the grace of God."

"And if, like me, you don't believe in God?"

"You become real only when you allow other people to be real. So much of the time, it's like other people are figures in a diagram. We navigate round them, through them, over them. But when you can see them with God's gaze, as entire beings, then there's hope for all of us."

"It sounds like hard work," I said.

Jun-su smiled. "Really, what work is more important than this?"

I did a great deal of research in order to understand Jun-su's story better, although my attempts to learn Korean were not very successful. I read works of history, biographies of the North Korean leaders, reports by human rights organizations, extracts from Jun-su's beloved comic books, and the only North Korean novel to have been translated into English: *Friend* by Paek Nam-nyong. I found it vague and abstract, shorn of the particularizing detail that brings fiction alive. I could feel the dead hand of the censor resting on Mr. Paek's shoulder, inhibiting his pen, if not his imagination. Reading it was like gazing through a very dirty window at an unfamiliar landscape. Yet in spite of that, I knew the world beyond it was inhabited by humans like me.

There's no shortage of accounts of life in the North Korean prison system. I read a lot of them. They reminded me of books by survivors of the Russian gulag and Nazi concentration camps. In order to survive, it was usually necessary to make moral compromises, steal food, harden your heart to the sufferings of others. When I read about starving prisoners salivating over the smell of burning human flesh from the crematorium, I imagined Jun-su in there. I wondered if, in the nine-year gap for which his encounter with Tae-il had become the most important symbol, there were just too many painful episodes for Jun-su to recall. Perhaps Jun-su was suffering from a kind of survivor's guilt. I wondered about his mother and father—and, of course, his abandonment of Su-ok.

At my wife's suggestion, I got in touch with David and Chibundo Kapsberger, who hosted me on a number of occasions at their lovely home in Islington. Professor Kapsberger was kind enough to show me some of the transparencies he took during his trip to the DPRK and share his reminiscences. He also clarified a number of points about the philosophy of Juche itself.

Fidel had recently moved to New York, but we spoke on the phone. He recalled little of the visit to North Korea, but he confirmed Joseph's account of their meeting in the early hours of January 2013. He had stayed in touch with Joseph during the years while he was resettling in the UK, occasionally traveling down to New Malden to have dinner with him. He even helped Joseph financially when he began his pharmacological training. Joseph's gratitude to Fidel was obvious in everything he said about him. Throughout Joseph's childhood, Fidel's name, inscribed on the flyleaf of the book, had been the token of something miraculous. Naturally, it had been one of the first things he looked for during his covert searches on the computers in Office 39. That was how he'd learned his address.

Towards the end of May, I finished a long project I'd been working on and I started thinking seriously about writing Joseph's story. I sent Joseph some text messages; he didn't reply. I didn't think anything of it at first, but then I became concerned.

I had a book that I had been meaning to give him. I'd come across it at Leisure Games in Finchley, a shop where I liked to browse on free afternoons. It was called *The Habitition of the Stone Giant Lord*, intentionally misspelled, and it was a compilation of homemade modules from the early years of role-playing games. To me, its manually typed pages evoke teenage years of rioting hormones and passionate involvement in the imaginary worlds of the game, arguing over crucial dice rolls with my friends Richard and Danna. I wondered how the book would touch Joseph. But I mainly thought it was a good excuse to renew our friendship.

All my efforts to get hold of him came to nothing. Finally I rang the Calvary Korean Church and asked to speak to the minister, Reverend Park.

There was a long hesitation at the other end of the line. "Jun-su is very ill," he told me. "We are praying for his recovery. He became sick. It's worse for him because of his preexisting heart ailment."

I felt both upset and strangely indignant. It would be cosmically unjust for Jun-su to survive all that danger and hardship only to fall victim now. He'd barely had a chance to begin his new life. And it seemed absurd to fixate on this detail, but hadn't the doctor at the sanatorium given him a clean bill of health? "I thought the heart murmur had cleared up," I said.

"So did he," said Reverend Park.

There was silence. It was brief, but long enough for me to register that outside my window was sunshine and children's laughter. The world seemed devastatingly unmoved by Jun-su's plight.

"It's been a very difficult time," the minister went on. "If you want to help, please join us in prayer."

"Is there anything else he needs?" I said. "How can I be of use? Medicine? Groceries? Money?"

I could hear Reverend Park fumbling with a piece of paper. "I'm going to give you his wife's number," he said. "You can ask her."

Susan Cho's contact details also connected me to a WhatsApp account. I searched it for clues to her identity. Unhelpfully, the photo was a Jesus and cross icon and the status was a verse from Philippians. I messaged that I had something for Joseph and that I would drop it off at their house. She replied with an address.

It was midsummer. The city had been sweltering in unseasonably hot weather since the spring.

Joseph lived in a block of ex-council flats on the outskirts of New Malden. The building was in good repair, but the stairwell was poorly lit and a bit cabbagey from uncollected warm rubbish. I climbed the stairs, left the book by the door, knocked, and withdrew. Joseph's wife opened it wearing a pale-green surgical mask. She was speaking loudly into a mobile phone in Korean and she sounded agitated. She picked up the package, waved a frantic thanks at me, and went back inside.

I didn't know what to make of it. My Korean was too rudimentary to know whether she had the accent of the North or the South. And I couldn't understand why Joseph hadn't told me he was married. Was it not important? Was it a source of embarrassment?

Descending the steps, I felt upset and perplexed, and also that my journey had been wasted.

I heard someone behind me. “I’m sorry,” said a lightly accented voice. “I didn’t get a chance to thank you. I’ve been trying to arrange childcare. Things have been very chaotic.”

“Is there any news about Joseph?” I asked.

To my enormous relief, she told me that Joseph was through the worst of his illness and that the doctors were hopeful he could come home soon.

I said I had a car and I’d be happy to pick him up. I told her I could be there within thirty minutes if she called.

Before she could respond, we were interrupted by a wailing sound from inside the flat. She went back and returned a few moments later carrying a baby. The child was about one and had a shock of spiky black hair and a grumpy, just-woken expression. But in that time of masks and protective plastic shields, it was nice to see an entire human face for a change.

“He’s very good-looking,” I said.

“She’s a she,” she said.

“My apologies. She’s very beautiful.”

“In Korean culture, it’s considered bad form to boast about yourself, your spouse, or your immediate family,” she said, but she didn’t contradict me.

“Perhaps that’s why Jun-su didn’t tell me about you and . . .”

“May,” she said. “At least, in English. In Korean, Mae-hwa.”

Mae-hwa, the winter plum, looked at me with undisguised

suspicion. Susan tickled her chin and the child snorted with pleasure. Turning to me, she said, "Jun-su is a bit paranoid. He still worries that the government will come after us."

"Are they that vindictive?"

"It depends. I was very close to the leadership in our country. My escape caused a lot of embarrassment to them."

As she was speaking, the child extended a hand and seized her mother's surgical mask, pulling it under her chin. I knew then for sure. She was exactly as he'd described: the alertness, the angular face, the hint of inner steel.

Su-ok had been left puzzled and hurt by Jun-su's rejection. Pragmatic and resourceful, she was also, perhaps inevitably, a romantic. In her mind, their love had been one of those remarkable relationships that feeds on its own strength and grows into an invisible monument that amazes everyone who witnesses it.

For a while, she bore the wound of rejection with the same self-mythologizing sense of destiny. It would be the pain that defined her. It was her punishment for having betrayed Jun-su. It made her real.

But when Jimi reported Jun-su's defection—and, after gentle pressing, revealed some of the details of the offer he'd made to him—she began to consider her future in North Korea.

Around the same time, the economic changes that had followed the Dear Leader's death began to go into reverse. Jang

Song-thaek, the Dear Leader's son-in-law who was credited with some of the liberalization that had taken place, was publicly denounced and executed. Depending on the accounts you read, he was either torn to pieces by dogs or obliterated with an antiaircraft gun.

The story of Su-ok's life in North Korea and her extraordinary escape—via the Gobi Desert to the South Korean consulate in Ulaanbaatar—merits an entire book. I fully expect her to write it herself one day.

"It was hard letting go," she told me. "Not the luxury. But the certainty. And Jun-su still frets about his mother. The truth is that every choice is a little death. You can't live to everything, you have to die to some things."

I went with Su-ok to pick up Jun-su on the day he was discharged from the hospital. We drove to St. George's and waited for him in the car park.

Su-ok went inside to fetch him and held the door as he came out. His illness had left him severely depleted. He was pale and his skin was drawn tight over his cheekbones.

We made an awkward salutation at the approved distance. "I appear to have made it out of another dungeon alive," he said, but his wryness clearly cost him a lot of effort.

During the drive home, they sat in the back seat in silence. I glanced round to check they were all right and I could see that they were holding hands. Jun-su had closed his eyes and Su-ok was stroking his cheek. He smiled weakly.

When we got back to their apartment, Su-ok helped him out of the car. I got out to close the passenger door and watched Jun-su walk unsteadily to the communal entryway, Su-ok a step behind. As they approached the doorway, Jun-su hesitated. Su-ok reached out to help him over the threshold and, for a brief moment, their silhouettes joined and they seemed to merge into a single figure. I felt something pricking my eyelids and turned my head to blink away tears. And when I looked again, they were gone.

# ACKNOWLEDGMENTS

This book owes an enormous debt to the many other writers who have covered aspects of life in North Korea. I would like to single out for special thanks Jieun Baek, author of *North Korea's Hidden Revolution*; Sujin Chun; Nigel Cowie; Andrei Lankov, whose sketches in *North of the DMZ* were particularly valuable for insight into the period during which this story takes place; Jihyun Park, whose memoir *Deux Coreénes*, jointly authored with Seh-Lynn, offers precious details of domestic life in North Korea; Alek Sigley; Son Byunggak; Daniel Tudor, author of *North Korea Confidential*; and Peter Ward.